Haunted Campers

True Ghost Stories

ALLAN ZULLO

Troll

To Kathy, the greatest companion ever
to hike mountains, ford streams, and blaze trails.

Copyright © 1996 by The Wordsellers, Inc.

Published by Troll Communications L.L.C.

All rights reserved. No part of this book may be reproduced or utilized in any form or by any means, electronic or mechanical, including photocopying, recording, or by any information storage and retrieval system, without written permission from the publisher.

Cover design by Tony Greco & Associates.

Cover illustration by Kersti Frigell.

Printed in the United States of America.

10 9 8 7 6 5 4 3 2 1

CONTENTS

Do Ghosts Roam the Countryside?

People say they have seen ghosts in all sorts of places: graveyards, caves, haunted houses... even the countryside. Campers have reported seeing phantoms in the woods, on the trails, and even by their campfire!

In many cases experts were called in to investigate these so-called hauntings. Usually the experts walked away baffled. All they knew for sure was that something weird had happened that could not be fully explained.

Haunted Campers is a creepy collection of stories about campers who have been haunted by spirits at or near their campsites. These eerie tales are inspired, in part, by real-life cases taken from the files of noted ghost hunters. The names and places in the stories have been changed to protect everyone's privacy.

Will a ghost haunt your tent the next time you go camping? You might think so after reading the spooky stories in this book!

BEWARE

THE SERPENT

T aylor Hobson untied the bandanna on top of his head and used it to wipe off the sweat that had been dripping into his blue eyes. He ran his fingers through his blond, shoulder-length hair, matted down by the humid summer air.

"What about this spot, Dad?" asked the 14-year-old, who was about hiked out after five hours on the trail.

Neil Hobson put his hand on Taylor's shoulder and told him, "Remember what I said about low-impact camping?"

"Yeah, I know. But this is such a pretty place. Nice grass right on the edge of the lake. I'd like to sketch some scenes from here."

"It's damp and full of mosquitoes, Taylor. Besides, the meadow by the water is fragile. The flowers and other plants are trying hard to survive. We don't want to make their task any harder by trampling them for a campsite."

"What about over there?" asked Taylor, pointing to a small clearing in the woods 50 yards (45 m) away. A large triangular-shaped boulder lay to one side.

After examining the spot, Neil announced, "It's got good drainage, filtered sun, and no vegetation. This will make an excellent campsite. The lake is still close enough for us to get our water. Remember, Taylor, the perfect camp is not made, it's found."

Unfortunately for Taylor he found a campsite that was anything but perfect. He never would have picked it had he known of the creepy ordeal he was about to face.

The slender, fair-skinned teen loved camping with his father. Taylor hardly saw him much during the week because Neil often worked late at the law firm. But once a month, the two would go camping in the wilderness so they could enjoy their hobbies—photography for Neil and art for Taylor. Whenever they went camping, Taylor brought along a large sketchbook and colored chalk. He liked to sit under a shade tree and capture the beauty of the countryside on paper.

After setting up their camp, Taylor, carrying his art supplies, wandered into the woods to look for an appealing scene to draw. Ten minutes later, he found it. Behind a thick growth of grass, dandelions, and goldenrod, he discovered a cluster of small stone grave markers. The thin, crudely chiseled stones, many topped with pale green lichen, leaned at odd angles. Age had darkened and weathered the markers, making it hard to see the names, dates, solemn sayings, and carvings etched on their fronts.

This is so cool—an old, long-forgotten cemetery, Taylor

thought as he tried to read the markers. *Sarah Whatley, 1791-1837, Gone But Not Forgotten...Josiah Hart, Born 1811, Died 1823, May He Suffer No More...Wow, what neat designs on these tombstones! I've got to do some grave rubbings.*

Taylor took out a sheet of paper and placed it over one of the gravestones. Then he rubbed lightly with a stick of black chalk. The design on the grave marker soon appeared on the paper. He made rubbings off of several other stones before he found a tombstone different from all the rest.

In the middle of the cemetery stood a gray marker that looked newer, sturdier, and less weathered than the others. Speckled with streaks of pink and flecks of white, it had no name, no date; only the words *Born* and *Died*. An unusual design had been carved into the top center of the tombstone— a coiled snake ready to strike.

Taylor pulled out another sheet of paper and did a rubbing of the design. When he finished, he noticed that a snake was carved into each of the first letters of the words *Born* and *Died*. He studied the rest of the tombstone, carefully sliding his fingers over its face to make sure there were no other markings that might have been eroded by time. *I wonder who this was meant for? Maybe it was—*

"Beware the serpent," whispered an eerie voice.

Taylor wheeled around, "Huh? Did somebody say something?" He scanned the cemetery but saw no one. "Dad, is that you?" *It wasn't my imagination. I definitely heard a man's voice. He sounded far away, and yet he wasn't shouting. Weird.*

Taylor began gathering his supplies when he heard a sound that sent shock waves through his body. He knew instantly what it was: *Rattlesnake! Don't panic. Stay still and try to spot him first.* Holding his breath, Taylor looked down at his feet, fearing the worst. He breathed a sigh of relief when he didn't see the snake. He looked to his left, his right, and then behind him. *There it is!* Shaking its rattle in the tall grass less than a yard (1 m) away from him, the snake slowly and menacingly began coiling up in an attack mode.

Terrified, Taylor leaped in the opposite direction and fled from the cemetery, running full speed back to the camp.

"Dad!" he shouted breathlessly. "A rattlesnake! I almost stepped on it!"

"Where?"

"In an old abandoned cemetery in the woods," Taylor replied, trying to catch his breath. "Oh, man, my heart is still racing. I hate snakes. They're the only things I don't like about camping."

"Taylor, remember, snakes aren't out to get you. They don't lie in ambush, and they don't go looking for trouble. They'll strike only if they're threatened. Just make sure you aren't seen as a threat to them. You have to be careful where you step, especially over logs and rocks."

"I had just put my things away when—" Taylor put his hand over his mouth and gasped. "Dad, just before I saw the snake, I heard a strange voice say, 'Beware the serpent.' There was no one around. And then a few seconds later I nearly stepped on the rattler!"

"The voice was your guardian angel warning you," Neil chuckled.

"Sure, Dad," said Taylor, rolling his eyes. "Got any other explanations?"

That night father and son crawled into their sleeping bags. Taylor didn't fall asleep right away. He was still reliving the close call he had with the rattler. In all the years he had been hiking and camping he had seen only four poisonous snakes—two rattlers, a copperhead, and a cottonmouth. For Taylor, that was four too many. But as his father had often told him, the snakes probably were more afraid of Taylor than he was of them. Eventually his thoughts turned to more pleasant subjects.

But during the night Taylor again heard that haunting, whispering voice from out of nowhere: "Beware the serpent."

"Dad," Taylor murmured. "Was that you?" Neil's response was a muffled snort. *Man, he's out cold. Where is this eerie voice coming from? Does it mean I'm going to see another snake?*

Taylor suddenly became aware of a weight, shaped like a thick sausage, on his sleeping bag draped across his thighs. Then he sensed movement. It began slithering toward his waist. *Oh, no, no, no! A snake!* Taylor's body went rigid with terror. He couldn't utter a sound.

Now it had reached his chest. Taylor could feel every muscle of the deadly reptile as first its front body slithered up, followed by its back end, then the front again. Soon it was only inches away from Taylor's exposed neck.

The petrified teen pictured in his mind what he could not see in the darkness of the tent: the snake's forked tongue flicking left and right, zeroing in on its target...the triangular-shaped head rising up...its cheeks swelling out with venom...its catlike pupils glaring at its helpless victim…its mouth gaping like a hinge. And now came the dreaded rattle—the sound of certain doom, the horrid warning that it was time to strike.

He's at my neck! He's going to sink his fangs into my Adam's apple, and I'm going to die a horrible death! I don't want to die! Noooooo!

Taylor's instinct for survival broke through his fear-induced paralysis. All in one motion, Taylor whipped off the unzipped side of his sleeping bag, leaped up, and in a throat-burning scream yelled, "Dad! Snnaaaakkke! Get out of the tent! Snnaaaakkke!"

Taylor jumped up and down like a maniac running in place, to keep his feet from touching the ground. Still in a frenzy, he tried to open the zippered flap to the tent.

Neil bolted up and immediately turned on a battery-operated lamp. "Where? Where's the snake!"

"On my sleeping bag!" cried Taylor as he fumbled with the zipper.

Neil grabbed a shirt to throw over the snake, but despite the light he couldn't find it. He quickly but carefully flipped over Taylor's sleeping bag. No snake. He slipped out of his bag and turned that over too. Still no snake. Neil checked under their clothes and in their boots. "Taylor, there's no snake in here."

"But he was on top of me! He was ready to strike at my neck. I felt him."

"The tent has a floor, the flap is zipped up, so a snake couldn't have gotten in here." Neil once again inspected every square inch of the tent, even looking for holes that a snake could have crawled through. He held up the lantern in front of his son. "My gosh, Taylor, you're shivering like it was 20 below zero (-29 C)."

"Dad, I heard that voice again. He said 'Beware the serpent.' And then I felt the snake crawling up my chest."

"Calm down, son, calm down. The tent is secure. It was a dream, that's all. A nightmare from seeing the rattler earlier today."

"But I could feel it on me. Every muscle in its body." Just recalling the incident made Taylor shudder.

The teen didn't sleep the rest of the night. Instead he lay still, waiting for the slightest movement, the softest sound, that would indicate the presence of a snake. He didn't want to hear a hiss or a rattle—or the voice.

At daybreak, while his dad was still asleep, Taylor stepped out of the tent. Normally, he never bothered using a hiking stick, but he remained spooked about the rattler in the cemetery and on his sleeping bag. So he found a stick that had a forked branch at the end to use as a weapon in case he met up with any more snakes.

Then Taylor tore the cardboard backing off his sketchbook. Using his pocket knife, he cut it in half. He rolled the halves and wrapped them around his ankles and lower calves. Then he pulled his hiking socks over the cardboard. It felt awkward, but at least it offered a defense if a snake tried to bite him while he was hiking.

Taylor had just finished getting dressed when his father came out of the tent. "Sorry about last night," said Taylor.

"You're not going to let this spoil our camping trip, are you?"

"It's all forgotten," Taylor fibbed.

They spent the day hiking through the woods and meadows, often stopping so Neil could take photographs while Taylor drew sketches. Taylor found it a little hard to draw because he had torn off the cardboard backing to his sketchbook. And it was somewhat uncomfortable walking with cardboard tubes around his ankles. But otherwise it was a pleasant day—especially because Taylor didn't see a single snake.

Shortly after dinner, Taylor, tired from a lack of sleep the night before, snuggled into his sleeping bag. Serenaded by the tree frogs and crickets, he fell fast asleep. A good, sound slumber until . . .

"Beware the serpent."

His heart pounding, Taylor gasped and shot out of his sleeping bag. He frantically turned on his flashlight and searched the floor of the tent. *I don't see any snake. Was I dreaming again?*

"Beware the serpent."

No way am I dreaming. This is real. Where is that voice coming from? Taylor wriggled into his jeans, threw on a shirt, and slipped into his hiking boots. Not wanting to wake his father, Taylor quietly left the tent, grabbing his trusty new hiking stick. The rays from the full moon shined through the trees to the forest floor like mini-spotlights on a stage. After searching the campsite for the source of the voice, Taylor started to head back into the tent when he heard horses trotting and snorting.

Soon he heard muffled conversation and the creaking and rumbling of wagons and buggies. Taylor followed the sounds into the woods for several minutes until he came to a rutted five-foot-wide (1.5-m) path. Standing off to the side behind an elm tree, Taylor watched as two men on horseback, dressed in black and holding candlelit lanterns, passed by. Four more similarly dressed men on horses followed them. Next came three horse-drawn buggies, each carrying a man and a woman. The men were dressed in dark suits and string ties; the women in long, high-necked black dresses. One lady had a veil over her face. Another was crying and dabbing her eyes with a hanky.

As he watched this odd caravan, Taylor grew increasingly frightened. His instincts told him to stay hidden. *What's going on? Who are these people? Why are they dressed that way?*

An enclosed black wagon rumbled by. Sitting alone up front on a high bench seat was a man dressed in black formal clothes and a black top hat. The side of the wagon had a horizontal oval window revealing a box inside it. Taylor knew instantly what it was—a coffin! In the moonlight, he read the white letters painted on the side of the wagon: KIMBALL FUNERAL PARLOR.

It's a funeral procession! They're all dressed up like the olden days. But what are they doing out here at this time of night? He looked at his watch. It was 11:45 P.M.

After the procession passed, Taylor followed it a short distance until it reached the abandoned cemetery he had discovered the day before. He crouched low and scooted behind a gravestone so he could see and hear what was going on.

To his surprise he saw a hole had been dug in the middle of the cemetery, in front of the tombstone where he had encountered the rattler. A pile of dirt lay to the side. As the others crowded around the hole, four burly men took the coffin out of the hearse. Aided by lanterns and the light of the full moon, they used ropes to gently lower the pine casket into the ground.

Taylor could hear sobbing, sniffles, and the clearing of throats. As the men stood with hats over their hearts, a preacher stepped forward and led them in prayer and a hymn.

"It is odd to hold a funeral service at midnight," the preacher told them. "But Brett requested it in his will. He always did things his way. That's what made him so special. And now let us hear from Brett's best friend, Lowell."

The preacher moved aside as a tall, lanky man in his twenties, nervously twisting his hat in his hands, addressed the gathering.

"They say the serpent is evil, that it crawls through life bringing fear and death to all whom it visits. Brett never felt that way. To him, snakes were beautiful and wise. They asked for nothing but to be left alone, to serve out their time on this earth doing what they were born to do. Brett used to say there are no gray areas for snakes: Cross them and they will strike; be respectful and they will do you no harm.

"Brett was fascinated by snakes his whole life. He knew more about those creatures than anyone else. That's why his death is so appalling. We all know how he met his end, trying to capture the biggest diamondback ever seen in these parts. He camped out by Snakehead Rock, that triangular-shaped boulder about ten minutes from here, and waited for that snake to make its move."

Snakehead Rock? thought Taylor. *Why, he's describing our campsite! The boulder next to our tent looks like the head of a*

16

snake. And it's a ten-minute walk from there to the cemetery.

"Brett fell asleep," Lowell continued, "and darned if that rattler didn't sneak out of his hole and climb onto Brett's chest. That wily snake must have known Brett was after him, because it bit him in the neck. Oh, sure, Brett had been bitten by snakes before, but not like this—not by a six-foot (1.8-m) diamondback in the neck. The pain must have been agonizing as his throat swelled up and he couldn't breathe. But at least it was over quickly.

"Who here imagined that Brett would die from the very kind of creature he loved so much? It's ironic, isn't it, that Brett should depart this life by the fangs of a rattler. But it was destined. What more fitting way to die for a snake lover whose last name was Serpent?"

When Taylor heard the dead man's last name, a chill slithered up his spine. *Did I hear right? Serpent? The eerie voice had said, 'Beware the serpent.' Maybe he meant the dead man. Maybe the voice was the dead man.*

When Lowell finished, each person stepped forward and, one by one, took a shovelful of dirt from the pile and gently tossed it into the burial hole. Then they quietly returned to their horses and buggies and headed back down the path.

Taylor remained hunched behind the tombstone, pondering what to do. *There has to be a connection between Brett Serpent and the voice I've been hearing. But what is it? I'd better follow them and see where they go. Maybe I can get some answers.*

When the hearse left the cemetery and entered into the shadows of the forest, Taylor scurried onto the path to catch up to the funeral procession. After running for a couple of minutes, he came to a halt. He peered into the forest, looking for the moving lights from the lanterns. He strained his ears to hear the horses or the creaking of the wagon wheels. *This is crazy. I should have caught up to them by now. I mean, they were only a few seconds ahead of me. There's no way they could have gone so far that I can't see or hear them.*

Suddenly a ghastly uneasiness crept over him. *Those people looked so weird. Where did they go?* He started to get scared. *What am I doing out here in the middle of the woods after midnight? This is the time when snakes are most active. I'd better get back to the camp now!* He turned on his flashlight and sprinted through the woods, worrying that the next step he took would be the one that landed squarely on the back of a rattlesnake. *Step here. No, there. Be careful, it could be on the other side of that log. What's that moving behind the rock? Do I keep running fast so a snake won't have time to bite me? Or do I walk slowly and carefully? Keep running! You'll get there sooner.*

Every step was torture. His flashlight swung wildly back and forth in search of the snake that he was sure would bite him. *Oh, why did I leave the tent? I had to be out of my mind. How much farther is it? I should be there by now. Wait, is that a snake? How about over there?*

Finally, Taylor reached the tent. He wanted desperately to wake up his father. But first he used his flashlight to check the inside of the tent for snakes.

"Dad! Dad! Wake up! I just saw a funeral!"

"Huh, what are you talking about? What time is it?"

Taylor looked at his watch. "It's 12:30 and —"

"Taylor, did you have another nightmare?"

"Dad, listen to me. This was no nightmare. It was real. Look at me. I'm sweating like I just ran the marathon. I was out by the cemetery, and you wouldn't believe what I saw."

Taylor excitedly described what he had witnessed. When he finished, he asked, "So what do you think, Dad?"

"I think you should go back to sleep."

"But Dad," Taylor complained.

"Okay. We'll go out to the cemetery in the morning and look around. If what you say is true, we'll find a freshly dug grave. Then we'll try to figure it out."

Like the night before, Taylor was unable to get back to sleep. The next morning he practically dragged his father to the cemetery. "I don't understand why, but the strange voice, the rattler, my nightmare, and the funeral are all connected," said Taylor.

Neil nodded. "Well, it's a possibility."

Taylor could tell from the tone that what his father was really saying was, "It's doubtful."

When they reached the cemetery, Taylor walked slowly through the tall grass, leery that the rattlesnake from two days ago might be lurking in the weeds. He held onto his fork-shaped hiking stick as he headed for the gravestone, just in case. "This is the one, Dad. Right here."

"Are you sure, Taylor? Look at the ground. It hasn't been disturbed."

"Something's not right. This is definitely the grave. Last night I saw a big hole here with a pile of dirt off to the left." However, they both could tell the ground hadn't been disturbed for a long time.

"I don't get it, Dad. I saw a funeral here last night, at this very gravestone."

His father kneeled down and examined the marker carefully, using his fingers to help him read the worn etchings. "Brett David Serpent," he said.

"I don't know his middle name," said Taylor.

"Well, it says it right here."

"What?" Taylor looked closely at the stone. It was hard to see but the full name was carved into the stone. And so were the dates of his birth and death: *January 13, 1827*, and *September 1, 1850*. A snake was carved into each of the first letters of his name and the months of the year.

Taylor grabbed Neil's arm. "Dad, his name and dates weren't on the stone before the funeral!"

"How do you know?"

Taylor reached into his backpack and unfolded the grave rubbing he had done earlier. "Look for yourself. I did this two days ago on this very tombstone. This rubbing proves that the only things on the stone were the serpent design and the words 'born' and 'died.' No name, no dates."

Taylor pulled out a sheet of paper and placed it over the stone and rubbed chalk over it. "Now look. The serpent design and name and dates are clearly seen on the paper. This stone was carved between Friday and today !"

"But the carving looks so old and worn."

"The people I saw at the funeral last night were dressed in clothes worn in the 1800s. Brett Serpent died in 1850. Dad, I was watching his funeral—a phantom funeral!"

"What makes you so sure?"

"The boulder next to our tent is shaped just like the head of a snake. Brett Serpent's friend said that Brett was camping by Snakehead Rock when he was killed, and that it was just ten minutes from here. I'll bet you I was sleeping in the exact same spot Brett was when the snake bit him. That's why I heard his ghost. That's why I relived the snake attack in my nightmare. And that's why I saw his phantom funeral!" Taylor's hands began to tremble. "Dad, can we get out of here?"

"Sure, Taylor, but do me one favor."

"What's that?"

"Keep your eye out for snakes."

CRY OF THE BANSHEE

Butterflies fluttered in Annie Pitts' stomach. As she stepped off the bus at Camp Sinnissippi, she surveyed the bustling crowd of kids, parents, and counselors scurrying, hugging, and waving. Then she grew scared.

This was the first time the pixie-sized ten-year-old had ever been to a sleep-away camp and the farthest she had ever been from home. To the curly-haired redhead, the lush, green mountains of New York's Catskills seemed like another country. Annie lived in a rundown apartment in Camden, New Jersey, with her widowed mother and older brother. She had expected to spend her summer playing in the park and at the local community center with her cousins. But her wealthy Aunt Lauren surprised her by arranging a two-week, all-expenses-paid stay at Camp Sinnissippi.

Annie expected to do things she had never attempted before—ride a horse, canoe, and hike in the woods. She hoped to meet new friends and have new experiences.

But she never could have imagined the terror she was about to face.

Annie's excitement about camp quickly turned to fear as the crowd of new kids swallowed her up. *I don't know where to go or who to see. What have I done? I don't belong here. What if I make a fool of myself? The other kids will make fun of me. I wish I were back home.*

"Hi, are you all right?"

Annie looked up and stared into the sparkling green eyes of a young woman whose long, pulled-back hair was so blond it almost looked white. Cocked slightly off center was a red and black Camp Sinnissippi cap worn by the counselors. The colors matched her T-shirt and shorts. The skin on her lean, muscular arms and legs was tinged red from the morning chill. "Can I help you?"

"Hi, I'm Annie Pitts, one of the new kids in camp. I guess I'm a little nervous."

"It's okay. A lot of tenderfeet are when they first arrive. But you'll love it here."

Annie bent down to pick up her suitcase. But when she stood up again, a different counselor stood in front of her. He directed her to a table in front of the main lodge. As luck would have it, Annie was assigned to Buckeye Cabin with nine Camp Sinnissippi veterans. They knew each other, came from the same ritzy New York suburb, and sported the latest fashions in clothes.

Although her cabin mates treated her politely, Annie felt like an outsider. After lights out, she tried to join their conversations, but often they chatted about people, places, and things she knew nothing about. Annie sensed that the self-appointed leaders of Buckeye Cabin, the catty MacIntosh sisters, looked down on her.

After the first few days, Annie continued to feel pangs of homesickness, especially when she wrote to her mother. Annie didn't realize how much she missed home, even her jerky brother Ronnie.

On the fifth night, Annie still had trouble sleeping. She decided to ignore the curfew and sneaked out of the cabin for a short walk at about midnight. With the moon nearly three-quarters full, she didn't need a flashlight. She had strolled about 200 yards (180 m) when she was startled by a soft voice.

"What are you doing up so late, Annie?" It was the friendly counselor Annie had met when she first stepped off the bus. "I hope I didn't scare you."

"I wasn't expecting anyone out here at this hour."

"Neither was I. So what are you doing?"

"I can't sleep."

"Those beds can be pretty hard. Is something else bothering you, Annie?"

"I guess I'm still a little homesick."

"That's normal. Heck, when I first went away to camp, I cried for a week because I didn't want to go. My parents had told me what a wonderful time I'd have. They were right, of course. But at first I kept wanting to go home. I guess I didn't have enough confidence in myself. I was afraid of new surroundings and new kids. But then I realized I was missing out on all sorts of fun. I could sit and mope or get into the swing of things. I chose to have a good time." The counselor raised her eyebrow and flashed a crooked smile. "But I didn't want to admit it to my parents. So you know what I did?"

"No, what?"

"I sent them a letter every day telling them that the camp counselors were mean and that they made us pull weeds, varnish tables, and scrub the mess hall floors. I wrote that they fed us dog food and bug juice."

"You didn't really," giggled Annie.

"Oh, yes I did. Then I really laid it on thick. I sprinkled my letters with water to blur some of the words. I circled the words and said, 'See? These are from my tears. I cry myself to sleep every night.'"

Annie laughed. "I can't believe you did that!"

"My parents called the camp director, Lee Ford, and said, 'What are you doing to my child?' He told them, 'Why, she's having a great time, playing softball, canoeing, and swimming. And, my goodness, she can eat for two football players.' So I got this stern letter from my parents telling me to knock off sending them stupid letters. I did stop—but I still had a little twinge of homesickness, because I really did miss them. Say, it's getting late. You'd better get back to your cabin."

"Wait," said Annie. "Before you go, what's your name?"

But the counselor had already disappeared into the darkness. *Next time I see her, the first thing I'm going to do is ask her name. And then I'll—*

"Who's out there?" asked a male voice.

"It's me, Annie Pitts," she replied. Annie looked over her shoulder and saw a counselor, who was carrying a flashlight, approach her.

"What are you doing out here?" he growled.

"I was just taking a walk. I couldn't get to sleep."

"What's your cabin?"

"Buckeye."

"Get back in there. You know the rules. No one is supposed to be outside after 10 P.M., especially alone. That'll be two demerits for Buckeye Cabin."

"Oh no, please don't do that," Annie pleaded. "The other kids will get on my case."

"You should have thought of that before you broke curfew. We have rules."

"But the other counselor didn't mind."

"What other counselor?"

After Annie described her, the counselor said, "I don't know who you're talking about. Now please get back to bed."

"Way to go, Annie," Carrie MacIntosh said sarcastically. "Now Buckeye Cabin can't win the Tip-Top Award."

"What's that?"

"The cabin that can make it through the week without a single demerit. You've blown it by getting caught breaking curfew."

Carrie's sister Cathy piped in, "Some of us have broken curfew before, but we never got caught." The MacIntosh girls shook their heads in scorn and walked off.

That afternoon the camp's ten cabins faced off in a swim meet. Annie wasn't looking forward to it. Although she knew how to swim, she wasn't very good or fast. But she was determined to do her best, hoping to make up for her demerits.

Each camper had to participate in at least one event. The Buckeyes decided that Annie would lead off in the relays and Carrie would anchor their team. Carrie, who was the best swimmer in camp, thought she could overcome Annie's lack of speed and outrace the others.

Each member of the four-girl team had to swim one complete lap. At the bang of the starter's gun, Annie belly-flopped into the pool. She paddled furiously but swam as though she were going against a stiff current. When she reached the other end, she misjudged the distance and smacked head-first into the wall. The pain caused her to yelp, and when she did, she took in a mouthful of water and started coughing. Annie stood up in the shallow end, gagging and spurting out water while her teammates screamed at her to start swimming. She tried but she kept coughing. The second-lap swimmers had caught up with Annie by the time she had completed her lap.

Despite a furious pace swum by Annie's teammates, the Buckeyes couldn't close the huge margin that Annie had created, and they finished last. They wouldn't let Annie participate in any of the other events—not that she wanted to anymore. Other than the relays, the Buckeyes performed quite well and finished second in the swim meet.

Any chance of Annie getting into the good graces of her fellow cabin mates had been sunk. "We would have won the camp championship if we hadn't finished last in the relays," whined Carrie in their cabin that night. All eyes turned to Annie, who sat on her bed with her arms wrapped around her knees, looking down at her feet. She knew they blamed her. And she felt more alone than ever.

As they lay in the dark, the other girls began talking about Pickney Point, a nearby cliff looking out over the Catskills. "I wish we could go up there," said one of the campers. "It's supposed to be the most beautiful sight in the state."

"They say a *banshee* lives up there, a scary female spirit who screams just before someone dies," Carrie claimed.

"I don't believe you," scoffed another camper.

"It's true," Cathy insisted. "Our family has known about it for years. The banshee is a pretty woman with long white hair and a gray hooded cloak. Her eyes are bloodshot from crying over the person who's about to die. Her cry sends chills through the heart of the bravest person. It's so awful that if you hear it, you know that you're the one who's going to die."

Carrie picked up the story. "Years ago a camper went up to Pickney Point and heard the banshee scream. He was so startled that he jumped back. He slipped and fell off the cliff and plunged to his death. The banshee cried harder than ever, knowing she had caused a young boy's death.

"Every time someone went up there to get the camper's hiking stick, they would get freaked out by the banshee's screams. She'd start wailing, and they'd run in panic and slip and fall off the cliff. That's why no one is allowed up on Pickney Point.

"The first camper's hiking stick keeps reminding the banshee of his death, and of the others who died. The only way to make it safe again at Pickney Point is to get the banshee to leave. She'll go once someone is brave enough to retrieve the hiking stick. Then campers will be allowed to go up there and enjoy the view."

"You're just making that up, Carrie," another camper sneered.

"No, I'm not. It's true."

"Hey, it's a full moon," said Cathy. "Why don't we go up there tonight and get the hiking stick?"

"Not me."

"Me neither."

"You're out of your mind."

Here's my chance to make things right, thought Annie. *If I can bring back the hiking stick from Pickney Point, they'll all be my friends. They'll see that I'm not a wimp who messes up. I can bring honor to Buckeye Cabin. What's the worst that can happen to me for breaking curfew? The camp could send me home early if I get caught. So what? I'm not having that great a time anyway.*

"I'll do it," Annie announced.

"What?" Carrie cackled. *"You?"*

"Yes, me. I'm not afraid of the banshee. I'll go up there and bring back the hiking stick. I've already been caught once for breaking curfew. There's no sense in one of you guys getting in trouble."

"Well, that's pretty brave of you, Annie," said Carrie. "Do you think you can do it?"

"No sweat."

"Super! Take the Munster Trail out back. After about ten minutes you'll see a 'No Trespassing' sign. That's the Pickney Point Trail. Good luck."

"Thanks." Annie tied her tennis shoes tight and threw a sweatshirt over her T-shirt. "See you guys soon." Then she slipped out the door and headed for the trail.

In the cabin the girls broke out in laughter, covering

their mouths so Annie couldn't hear them.

"Where did you ever come up with such a story?" a cabin mate asked the two sisters.

"We're just gifted I guess," Carrie replied smugly.

One of the girls threw a pillow at Carrie. "You're so modest, Carrie."

"But what if Annie goes to Pickney Point and she gets hurt?" asked another camper. "No one is supposed to be up there because it's dangerous."

"Yeah, maybe we should go after her," chimed another cabin mate.

"What?" Carrie sneered. "And spoil all the fun? No way. She won't go up there, anyway. She'll be too scared. As a matter of fact, I'll bet you she won't make it to the 'No Trespassing' sign. Listen, if she's not back here in an hour, we'll get a counselor."

But by then they would be fast asleep.

When Annie was far enough away from the camp, she flipped on her flashlight and marched up to the sign warning hikers to stay away from Pickney Point. She took a couple of deep breaths and headed up the trail. It was a lot steeper than she thought. Grunting and sweating, Annie worked her way up by clutching roots and rocks on the path.

After 15 minutes of climbing, she stopped to rest. *What am I doing out here?* she asked herself. *Am I crazy? What if the banshee starts screaming? I could fall off the cliff and die. For what? A stupid stick? Who cares what those Buckeyes think anyway? Hey, what if there is no such thing as a banshee? What if Carrie and Cathy made it up? I'd look like even more of a fool. I know what I'll do. If I don't find the hiking stick,*

I'll get an old branch, tear off the leaves, and make one.

Annie climbed on with renewed enthusiasm, ignoring the occasional slips and stumbles. Twenty minutes later she reached the top, a huge flat rock twice the size of Buckeye Cabin. Surrounded on three sides by tall trees, Pickney Point sloped downward at a slight angle before it ended in a drop-off to the valley 1,000 feet (300 m) below. A rush of excitement flowed through Annie's veins—she had reached the summit, something no other camper had done.

Annie raised her arms in triumph and glanced at the moon. Thin clouds streaked across the sky. For a moment she imagined they formed a squadron of witches flying on brooms.

The breeze had picked up considerably, causing the pines to whistle eerily in the night. Annie searched the cracks and crevices of the rock, looking for the dead camper's hiking stick. *Hurry up,* she told herself. *Find the stick and get out of here before the banshee starts screaming. And don't panic if she does scream. Oh, I hope she doesn't. Where is that stick? I've looked everywhere. Maybe if I get closer to the edge—*

"Aieeeeeeeee!"

The banshee!

Annie spun around and saw a figure running toward her from the far side of the rock! As it came closer, the moonlight revealed a woman with long, white hair in a gray hood, her arms outstretched, shrieking at Annie. *It's true!* thought a terror-stricken Annie. *There really is a banshee! Get out of here, Annie, before you die!*

"Aieeeeeeeee!"

Annie made a desperate lurch to the right. But her left foot caught a crack in the rock, and she tumbled onto the hard surface. *The banshee is coming closer. I've got to get out of here!* Annie scrambled to her feet. *The banshee is gaining on me!* Blindly trying to run, Annie failed to notice the loose stones. Her feet gave way, and she landed on her belly, scraping her hands and chin.

Suddenly she began to slide on the sloping rock, down toward the edge of the cliff face. *I'm going to die! I heard the banshee and now I'm going to die!* In desperation, Annie clawed at the rock, trying to find something, anything to grasp to stop her fall. But she was slipping faster and faster to what seemed like certain doom.

"Noooooooo!"

Her fingers rubbed raw from trying to brake her sliding, Annie helplessly skidded to the edge of the rock. She screamed in panic when she felt her feet dangle over the side and then, a heartbeat later, she plunged off it. But the side angled out slightly, and miraculously Annie was able to grab onto a bush that was growing out of the cliff face, stopping her fall into oblivion. She held on for dear life, hoping the bush would not give way under her weight. Her feet frantically felt around for a crack or small hole to rest.

Suddenly she found footing on a tiny ledge wide enough to hold only the tips of her shoes. With her arms stretched high, clutching the bush, and her toes barely touching the ledge, Annie caught her breath. She wanted to take deep breaths, but she was afraid that if her chest expanded, it would shove her off the ledge.

Her head was turned to the right and pressed so firmly against the cold, mossy cliff face that she could feel her pulse throbbing in her temple. Slowly she looked down but couldn't see the bottom in the darkness. She glanced to her left and right. Small rocks and thin ledges jutted from the cliff face. She looked up and realized how far she had fallen. It was about 30 feet (9 m).

It's hopeless, Annie thought. *There's no way I can climb back up. I don't know how to climb down the side of the cliff. What do I do? No one is going to hear me if I scream. I've got to wait until morning. But how can I hold out that long? My arms are aching. If I put them down, I'll fall and die. Maybe I should just give up, let go, and end this misery. But I can't. I'm too young to die. How could I have been so stupid? How could I have been—*

"Annie! Thank goodness you're alive!"

Annie looked up. The hooded, white-haired woman stared down at her from the top of the edge.

"Oh my gosh!" whimpered Annie. "The banshee!"

"Annie. Don't move. I'm going to help you." The voice sounded familiar, soothing, and comforting. Seconds later, Annie felt a hand on her shoulder. "Stay calm."

Annie turned her head to the right and saw the friendly counselor whose name she didn't know. The young woman was spread-eagled against the cliff face, her toes jammed on the tiny ledge.

"How did you get down here so fast?" asked Annie.

"No time to explain."

"Are you the banshee?"

"You can call me that."

Annie took a closer look. That was no hooded cloak the woman was wearing; it was a hooded Harvard sweatshirt. The long hair wasn't white; it was light blond.

"I tried to warn you, but I think I scared you instead," said the counselor. "I'm so relieved you're alive."

"Am I going to die?"

"Not if I can help it. Now stay cool and do exactly as I tell you, okay?"

Annie nodded.

"We need to walk across the cliff face for about 100 feet (30 m) until we come to a vertical crack in the side. From there we can crawl up to safety."

"But this ledge is so narrow," Annie said.

"You've got to do it. It's your only hope. Now don't look down. Just stay focused. Slowly let go of the bush with your left hand and let it slide down the face of the rock until you find something to grab onto."

Annie did what she was told.

"Great," the counselor said. "Do the same with the other hand. Good. Next, move your right foot up and over until you feel another little ledge. You're doing just fine."

Inch by agonizing inch Annie worked her way across the face of the cliff. Her mind was so focused on finding the next hole or rock to grasp that she had no concept of time or distance. Seconds seemed like minutes; inches seemed like feet. Fear and concentration had sucked all the moisture out of her mouth and drenched her face in sweat.

She had never been so scared in her life. She knew that one false slip, one small miscalculation, one loose rock, would send her to her death. She couldn't cry or even speak. Every tense muscle in her body ached, especially her shoulders and the back of her calves. Her hands, wrists, and ankles trembled.

At times Annie felt she couldn't go any farther, but the counselor coaxed her into taking one step at a time. "Just one more step. Good. Okay, now move your right hand down a few inches. There, hold onto that rock and push off with your left foot. Good . . ."

Painstakingly, they made their way like flies on a wall across the cliff face. After what seemed like an eternity to Annie, they finally reached the large vertical crack in the cliff face. The crack was wide and deep enough for both of them to squeeze into. For the first time since she had fallen off the edge, Annie took a deep breath. And then another one. They had never felt so good.

"You did great, Annie, just great," the counselor said. "Now rest a bit and try to relax. The worst is over."

Annie closed her eyes and wept softly.

"Now here's what we're going to do next," said the counselor. "You're going to press your back against one wall of the crack and push your feet against the opposite wall. You're going to climb in this sitting position. Okay?"

"I don't know if I can do that," Annie said fearfully.

"Yes you can, Annie. I'll be pushing you from underneath. Let's go."

Gathering all the strength she could muster, Annie slowly inched her way upward. Ten feet (3 m), 15 feet (4.5 m). Her thighs were burning and her back was searing from pushing and scraping against the rock. But she kept going. At 20 feet (6 m), she hit her head on a stick that had lodged in the crack. Annie yanked on it until it came free and landed on her chest. She was about to toss it aside when she noticed a face had been carved on it. "This looks like a hiking stick," she whispered.

"It is, Annie. Keep going. Another ten feet (3 m) and you'll be there. You're doing wonderfully!"

Annie didn't know why, but she held onto the stick as she grunted and groaned toward the top. Twenty-five feet (7.5 m). Finally, Annie's head stuck out above the top of the crack. "I'm almost there!" she shouted. "I can see the top of the rock!" Annie tossed the hiking stick up onto the rock surface, grabbed the edge, and pulled herself out.

"I did it! I did it!" Annie threw herself down on all fours and kissed the cold rock. Then she sobbed. All the pent-up fear and tension from knowing she could have died at any moment came pouring out in a torrent of tears and wails. She cried until there was not another tear to wring out. And then Annie passed out.

"There she is! I think she's alive!" shouted Lee Ford, the camp director. He dashed over to Annie, who was still sprawled on the top of the rock.

"Wha—what happened? Where am I?" Annie asked groggily as she squinted in the morning sun.

"You're on the top of Pickney Point and you're safe!" Lee replied with relief. "Your cabin mates told us where to find you. Are you hurt? Can you move your arms and legs?"

Annie nodded and sat up. "I think I'm okay." Holding onto the hiking stick with one hand and Lee's arm with the other, Annie stood up and shakily walked over to the trees where it was safer. She leaned against a trunk while the other counselors checked her bruised body.

At Lee's prodding, Annie sheepishly confessed the reason she had gone to Pickney Point. Then she explained in detail how that wonderfully nice camp counselor—whose name she still didn't know—came to her rescue and guided her to safety.

"Counselor?" Lee asked. "Annie, no counselor was up here last night."

He looked at the others. "Do you know who she's talking about?" They all shook their heads.

"You might be a little confused from your ordeal," Lee told her. "Let's go back to camp."

Annie got up and took a few steps. "Oh, I almost forgot my lucky hiking stick."

When Lee picked it up for her, he noticed a carving on it of a woman with long hair flowing behind her. Her mouth was open as if she were shouting. Below the figure were the initials J. A. "Annie, where did you get this?"

"In the big crack I climbed out of. It was stuck in there."

"I don't believe it!" raved Lee, showing it to the others. "It's Jamie Arnold's hiking stick! I gave it to her for being named the year's top counselor."

"Who's Jamie Arnold?" Annie asked.

"She was a wonderful counselor," replied Lee. "One of the best ever. She was fantastic with kids. Very understanding. A big heart. She loved working with campers. She would have been a senior at Harvard this fall if it hadn't been for the tragedy."

"What tragedy?"

"About five years ago Jamie was leading a group of hikers up to Pickney Point. One of the campers got too close to the edge and slipped. He fell about 30 feet (9 m) down the cliff face, but fortunately landed on a narrow ledge. Jamie found a way to get to him and managed to guide him to the vertical crack you climbed out of. But then he panicked and started screaming and flailing his arms. He knocked her back, and she lost her footing and fell to her death."

"Oh, how awful," said Annie. "And so weird. What happened to me was like a replay, only with a happy ending." She paused. "So who saved my life?" Recalling her rescuer she said, "She had long, white-blond hair and was wearing a Harvard sweatshirt. And when I asked her if she was the banshee, she said, 'You can call me that.'"

Lee's hand slid down the hiking stick as he slumped to the ground, stunned by what he had just heard. "Annie, you just described Jamie perfectly."

"But she's dead," said Annie. "It couldn't have been her unless she was a...a..." Her voice trailed off. She couldn't bring herself to say the word ghost. "I think I'd better sit down too. I'm feeling kind of shaky."

"I'm blown away by what you said about the banshee," Lee said. "You see, Jamie had an incredibly strong voice. She won the camp yelling contest two years in a row. Her voice was so loud and high-pitched, we used to call her The Banshee. In fact, the carving on this hiking stick is a banshee."

If there was any doubt in Annie's mind who had saved her, it was put to rest. *I was rescued by the Banshee of Pickney Point!*

THE REBEL

GHOSTS

When their mother dropped off 16-year-old Mike Manley and his 15-year-old brother Joe at a Tennessee state park for a weekend camping trip, she was worried about their safety.

But the burly brothers, who wanted to get in one last weekend of camping before fall football practice started, joked about her concerns. After all, their parents had been taking them camping ever since they were in diapers. The boys loved the outdoors and had great respect for Mother Nature's beauty—and her wrath.

"Don't worry, Mom," said Joe as he took their camping supplies out of the car trunk. "We're experienced campers. We can look out for ourselves. What could happen?"

If they only knew.

What awaited the Manley brothers was beyond their wildest dream—or, to put it more accurately, their scariest nightmare.

* * *

Mike and Joe pitched their tent at one of the primitive campsites off a seldom-used path across from a stand of poplar trees. Then they set out on a six-mile (9.6-km) round-trip hike.

About a mile (1.6 km) from their camp they came across a middle-aged man. He wore a floppy hat, blue overalls, a plain white shirt, and scuffed-up tan boots. Over his shoulder he carried a Springfield rifle, a muzzle-loading, one-shot gun popular during the Civil War.

"Morning, boys," greeted the man. He sized them up, wrinkled his nose, and asked, "You from around here?"

"Nashville," Mike replied.

"Rebels, huh? Seen any action?"

"Pardon?"

"For crying out loud, the Civil War is spilling blood everywhere across this great state. What are you, *deserters*?"

"Tell you what, sir," said Mike, growing wary of the stranger. "We're going to continue on our hike. Have a nice day."

"Hold on, sonny," ordered the man, taking the rifle off his shoulder, but careful not to point it at the boys. "You need to hear what happened up yonder yesterday in the battle at Stones River."

"Mike, what are we going to do?" Joe whispered. "We're standing here in front of a crazy man with a gun."

"Let's humor him," said Mike. "Don't do anything to annoy him."

They sat on a nearby log as the man launched into his story. "My name is John Bellows. You know, some folks in

Tennessee are fighting for the Union and others have thrown their lot with the Confederacy. Families are getting all torn up. Brother against brother. Friend against friend. Personally, I don't much care which side wins, just as long as they leave my little farm alone."

"Let me get this straight," said Joe. "Are you telling us that the Civil War is going on *now*?"

"Sure as shooting."

"But that ended over 130 years ago!"

The boys turned to each other and nodded as if to say, "He's definitely crazy."

Bellows ignored their mocking attitude and continued. "I witnessed the Battle of Stones River yesterday. At one of the battle fronts, the Rebels from the Third Kentucky were advancing on a Union regiment. The soldiers from these two regiments once lived in the same area. Former friends and neighbors were now pitted against each other as enemies. But when they recognized one another, they stopped shooting.

"Dang if they didn't begin bad-mouthing each other, saying the most vile things. It was hard to tell which side would win the war of words, because neither side was very good at it.

"Finally they got tired of name-calling and went back to fighting. They picked up their muskets and charged into each other. But they didn't shoot. Instead, they used their muskets as clubs. When that didn't work, they threw down their weapons and fought with their fists. What a sight! Hundreds of soldiers rolling around on the ground, gouging, scratching, and punching in wild abandon.

"The Rebels were getting the best of the Yanks until the Ninth Ohio came to the rescue of the Union men and captured the Rebs. The prisoners were marched to the rear. Soon they were chatting and joking with their old friends and neighbors just like the days before war broke out."

Bellows scratched his bushy brown sideburns. "I could carry on all day, but I best be moving on. But if you want to see the Battle of Stones River, be here tomorrow at noon. See you around."

Bellows stood up and started to walk away, leaving the boys stunned. Mike murmured, "Either that guy is crazy, or...or—"

"Or he's a ghost!" Joe declared.

Just then Bellows turned around. "You must be wondering whether I'm a nut or a ghost. Am I right?"

"Oh, no, sir, nothing like that," Joe fibbed.

"Well, I'm neither. I belong to a group of Civil War buffs. Tomorrow we're all getting dressed up as Rebels and Yankees to reenact the battle. I was acting out my part for you. So what did you think?"

"Pretty good," said Mike. "It's nice to know you're not a nut."

"Or a ghost," Joe added.

"Well, I'm not so sure you won't see a ghost or two out here this weekend," said Bellows. "Spirits of dead soldiers are known to roam battlefields. People say that battle reenactments sometimes stir up the ghosts. Personally, I've never seen one. I doubt they even exist. But then, you never know."

* * *

That night Joe was awakened by a soft sound. He glanced over at Mike, who was still asleep. Joe got up and stepped out of the tent, listening for the sound again. As he walked toward the tree line, he suddenly had an uneasy feeling, the kind you get when you're alone but think you're not.

CREAK, CREAK...CREAK, CREAK.

What could be making that sound? Joe wondered. He held his breath so he could listen better. He heard a platoon of crickets chirping in unison and the whistle of a gentle breeze. But he couldn't identify that creaking noise. *It sounds like rope being pulled tight. Or maybe rope rubbing against something. Where is it coming from?*

CREAK, CREAK...CREAK, CREAK.

Joe followed the noise to the stand of poplar trees across from the campsite. He still couldn't find the source.

Maybe it's just a branch rubbing against another branch. He started back toward the tent when, out of the corner of his eye, he noticed movement.

CREAK, CREAK...CREAK, CREAK.

Inexplicably, Joe felt a sickening sensation in the pit of his stomach, as if his body was preparing him for an unpleasant shock. He could almost hear his brain tell his head not to glance up. But he had to look.

Slowly Joe tilted his head and gazed at the sturdiest of the poplars looming about ten feet (3 m) to his left. *Something is hanging from the tree! Two things! No, four things!* Joe reeled back, not knowing what they were. As his eyes adjusted to the night, the objects came into clearer focus...and then his mind went numb with shock.

Dangling about three feet (1 m) off the ground were two pairs of human legs! Joe didn't want to look anymore, but he couldn't stop himself. His eyes followed the legs to the waist, then to the torso and finally to the head of each figure.

Two men hanging by ropes around their necks were spinning ever so slowly in the breeze. Their hands were tied behind their backs. The slumped head of one of the men turned toward Joe. His face, twisted in agony, gave mute testimony to his awful death. A blindfold that obviously had been wrapped around his eyes had slipped down to his chin. A blindfold on the other victim still covered his face.

CREAK, CREAK...CREAK, CREAK.

The mysterious sound Joe had heard were the ropes rubbing against the thick branch of the poplar tree.

So great was his shock that it was a full minute before Joe could move a muscle or even breathe. When he was finally able to regain his senses, he tried to scream. At first nothing came out of his throat. He tried again. *"Ahhhhhhhhh!"*

Joe turned to run, but he tripped over a rock and sprawled on the ground.

"Joe? Joe!" shouted Mike as he stumbled out of the tent. "Is that you? What's the matter?"

"Dead men!" blurted Joe, scrambling to his feet. "Two men are hanging by their necks from that tree."

The words struck Mike like a punch to the stomach. He aimed the flashlight toward the tree. The beam of light followed the trunk of the tree up to the branch.

"I don't see anything," said Mike.

Joe grabbed the flashlight from Mike and aimed it at the

big branch where he had seen the hanged men. But there were only leaves and smaller branches. Joe quickly turned the light to the other big branches and then other trees. Again, no bodies.

"I—I don't understand," stammered Joe. "I swear I saw two men hanging by their necks. I even heard the rope creaking on the branch. I walked right by them. I could have reached out and touched them. They had dark-colored shirts, pants, and boots. Mike, it was awful. I saw one of the dead man's faces. I'll never forget that horrible look." Joe began to shiver.

"Joe, get a grip on yourself. You were probably sleepwalking and had a nightmare."

"Do you think so? Gee, I hope you're right. But it seemed so real. It's hard to believe it was only a dream. I'm sorry I got you up, Mike."

"Forget it. Let's get some sleep."

When they returned to their tent, Joe's heart continued to beat overtime. There was no way he could fall back to sleep.

The next morning a thick fog shrouded the area in a drab gray as the brothers munched on a breakfast of granola bars, peanut butter sandwiches, and purified water. Joe still couldn't get that horrible, vivid nightmare out of his mind.

"Hey, Joe, do you hear thunder?" asked Mike.

"Sounds more like galloping horses."

"Could be. Wait—I think I hear people talking on the other side of our camp."

Straining their ears, the boys overheard a conversation coming through the fog.

"Colonel Baird, I'm Colonel Austin and this is Major

Dunlap. We're inspectors-general. Our mission is to inspect the outposts and defenses of the Union troops in this area. Here are our papers from General Rosecrans and from the War Department in Washington."

"These papers all look in order. I'll have an officer escort you around the perimeter."

"Thank you for your cooperation, Colonel."

The conversation ended. Joe and Mike listened for any more voices but heard only songbirds.

"What do you suppose that was all about, Mike?" Joe asked.

"Well, one of them mentioned the Union army, and I remember from history class that General Rosecrans commanded Union troops in Tennessee during the Civil War. I'll bet you those Civil War buffs are practicing their reenactment for later today."

"Of course, Mike, that's what it is."

"I wonder why we couldn't see them. Even though the fog is pretty thick, they sounded like they were standing close enough for us to see them. It doesn't —"

Mike was interrupted by an excited high-pitched voice with a strong southern drawl. "Colonel Baird, those two men are Rebel spies! I know one of them. He ain't no Colonel Austin. He's Lieutenant Charles Peters of the Confederacy. He's from my hometown!"

"Corporal Kramer, are you positive?"

"I know for a fact, Colonel. They're spies!"

"Sergeant Hancock. Get four of your men and bring those two officers to me immediately. If they make any suspicious moves, shoot them."

The boys listened for more of this battlefield saga, but the voices remained silent. The brothers searched futilely in the fog for the men.

After a few minutes Mike told Joe, "No way anyone is going to have a reenactment in this pea soup."

"I'd sure like to know the end of the story," said Joe. "I wonder what happened to the two spies."

"They probably were hanged."

Joe broke out in a cold sweat. He clutched his brother's arm. "Mike! My nightmare—the two men hanging from a tree. I just remembered they were wearing clothes that looked like Union officers' uniforms. Do you think there's a connection?"

Before Mike could answer, a gunshot rang out.

"Nobody is supposed to be hunting out here," Mike grumbled.

"Maybe it was one of those Civil War buffs shooting a blank."

"Yeah, that's probably it."

But then in the near distance they heard a man in a squeaky, high-pitched voice cry out, "I didn't mean to do it! Oh, lordy, I didn't mean for it to turn out this way!"

"That sounds like the corporal we heard earlier," said Joe. "What was his name?"

"Kramer. He sounds hurt. Let's find him. I think the voice is coming from behind those trees."

As they hurried in the fog the brothers heard the man wail, "Oh, why, why, why! How could I let this happen?"

Using their ears as their guides, the boys found a man in his twenties on his knees, crying and hunched over so far that his head was nearly touching the ground. His whole body shook after each sob.

"Sir, are you all right?" asked Joe.

The man jerked up. His scraggly brown hair drooped over his forehead and ears and into his wet sad eyes. He was dressed in the blue uniform of a Union soldier.

"Sir," Joe repeated. "Are you okay?"

"I've been shot," the soldier grimaced. He turned around to show a bloody spot in the upper part of his stomach, just below his rib cage.

"Oh my gosh," Joe exclaimed, "we need to get you to a hospital!"

"Don't bother," the soldier moaned. "It won't do any good."

"But you could bleed to death."

The soldier chuckled. "Bleed to death, huh? That's a good one."

"What's so funny?" Joe asked.

"Life," muttered the soldier, "and death."

"You need help," said Joe as he and Mike took a few steps closer to the soldier. He waved them off. "I don't need your help. It's too late for that."

"Say," said Mike, snapping his fingers. "You're one of those Civil War buffs, right? You're just acting."

"I don't know what you're talking about," said the soldier, wincing from the pain. "I'm Corporal Emmit Kramer of the Sixth Kentucky Cavalry."

"Just tell us if you've been shot or not," said Mike. "We don't know whether you're playing a role or are really hurt."

"Can't you see I'm suffering?"

"So let us help you," Joe pleaded.

"Too late," Kramer groaned.

The boys looked at each other helplessly. They stepped away from Kramer and planned their next move. "What do you think we should do, Mike?"

"Let's play along with him. It's just an act—a good one too. Maybe we'll learn more about the Civil War."

Kramer crawled to a tree, leaned against it, and kept his hands pressed over his bleeding wound. "Have you ever snitched on someone and then regretted it?"

"I—I guess so," Joe replied, "when we were little kids in grade school."

"I wish I could say that," said Kramer. "Then maybe they wouldn't have died."

"Who are you talking about?" asked Mike.

"Austin and Dunlap. Only their real names were Peters and Orton."

"The two Rebel spies we heard earlier," Joe whispered to Mike.

Kramer began sobbing again. "Why didn't I keep my trap shut? Oh, the heartache I've brought to my family. But what could I do?"

"Kramer, what happened?" asked Mike.

"I squealed on them!" Kramer bawled. "I knew they were spies, and after I told Colonel Baird, he had them arrested. They were very upset and said they strongly objected to such treatment of Union officers. Colonel Baird told them of his suspicions, and said that if they were indeed who they claimed to be, they shouldn't mind his extra precautions. The colonel immediately telegraphed General Rosecrans, who replied that he knew nothing of the men and that he had not ordered any inspectors-general to the area.

"Then the colonel brought me in to confront them. The colonel asked me point blank, 'Do you know these men?' I felt compelled to tell the truth. I had no choice. I pointed to Colonel Austin and said, 'He is Charles Peters, an officer of the Confederate Army. I have known him all my life.'

"Charles looked me in the eyes and hissed, 'How could you betray me like this?' Before anyone could move, he whipped out a pistol he had hidden in his boot and shot me. The guards overpowered him and led him and his partner, Ray Orton, away. Even though I was hit, I ran off. I couldn't bear to be around the camp. Now I'm wracked with guilt. As surely as I fingered Charles, I might as well have pulled out my sword and thrust it through his heart."

"But you were only acting as a good Union soldier should," said Joe. "You had to do it, or else you could have put your whole division in jeopardy."

"You don't understand," cried Kramer. "Charles was my half-brother! We grew up together. We shared the blood of my mother. And he was going to marry the sister of my best friend."

"What happened to Charles and his partner?" asked Mike.

Kramer buried his head in his bloody hands. Then his trembling finger pointed to the big poplar tree behind them. The boys turned around and gasped.

Through the swirling gray mist they saw two figures dangling from the tree. The brothers rubbed their eyes, unwilling to accept at first what they were seeing.

"It…it's two men hanging by their necks!" stammered Joe. "Just like my nightmare! Right down to the blindfold over the face of one of them! Only now I don't think it was a nightmare. I think it was real!"

"Joe, it can't be," claimed Mike, shaking his head in bewilderment. "It just can't be!"

"What will we do, Mike?"

"We need to get a closer look." Suddenly Mike clapped his hands and grinned. "I know who they are. They're dummies for the reenactment."

"But, Mike, what if they're not? I've never seen a dead body before. I don't know if I have the stomach for it."

"Then I'll go. You stay here with Kramer."

Just then Kramer slumped to the ground and uttered a frightening moan. His chest heaved once before his body went limp.

"Kramer!" shouted Joe. "Corporal Kramer!"

Joe bent down to lift him up. But to his incredible shock, his hands went right through Kramer's body! Joe screamed and backed away. "Mike, did you see that? Am I having another nightmare?"

"I almost feel that *I'm* the one having it. This kind of thing doesn't happen in real life."

"What is he, a ghost?"

Half of Mike's brain urged him to flee. The other half wanted him to stay long enough to confirm what he had just seen with his disbelieving eyes. The shuddering teen bent down and, with his index finger, tried to touch the lifeless body. His finger went into Kramer's chest without any resistance. All Mike felt was a slight chill. Then his quivering hand swiped effortlessly through Kramer's head. "Oh, my gosh, he *is* a ghost!"

Mike yelled the words with such fear that both brothers started running blindly toward their campsite. But then Joe grabbed Mike, pointed to the poplar tree, and shouted, "Look! The two men are gone!"

They ran up to the tree. Mike climbed it and examined the branch. "I don't see any rope burns on the branch. The bark hasn't been damaged."

"Quick, Mike, let's get back to Kramer."

But even before they got there, they knew what they would find—nothing. Kramer too had disappeared.

As they headed back toward their campsite, they saw a figure walking in the fog. "Another ghost?" asked Joe.

"Hello!" It was Civil War buff John Bellows in uniform. "Everything okay?"

"Not exactly," replied Mike. "Are you guys practicing a scene for the reenactment?"

"No," said Bellows. "The whole thing was called off because of the bad weather. We'll try again next week."

"Have you ever heard of two Rebel spies named Colonel Austin and Major Dunlap?" Joe asked. "Their real names were Charles Peters and Ray Orton, and they were hanged."

"No."

"What about a corporal named Emmit Kramer?"

"Doesn't ring any bells," Bellows answered. "Why all the questions?"

"Let's say we may have just seen a piece of history," said Mike. "A very sad piece."

The Manley brothers remained bewildered days after their incredible camping experience. Did the spies they saw and the soldiers they heard really exist? If so, that could only mean one thing: They were battlefield ghosts.

Then one day shortly afterward, Mike phoned Bellows, who suggested the brothers meet him at the local historical society. Once there, the three of them rummaged through old documents for hours until Bellows shouted, "I found it!"

He pulled out a yellowed, handwritten piece of paper dated June 9, 1863. It was a Union army account of the execution of two Rebel spies—Charles Peters, alias Colonel Austin, and Ray Orton, alias Major Dunlap. The paper described everything that Joe and Mike had seen and heard in the fog. The brothers slumped in their chairs, stunned by further evidence that they had encountered spirits from the Civil War.

The account said that one of the soldiers, Emmit Kramer, had fingered his half-brother, Charles Peters, who then, in a rage, shot him. Kramer was later found dead outside the Union encampment.

According to the document, the spies were given a trial and sentenced to death. They wrote letters to their friends and family, enclosing their valuables. Then they were hung from a poplar tree. Both men were buried in the same grave—companions in life, companions in infamy, and now companions in death.

THE SPECTER OF
NUMBER NINE

Ah, isn't great to be out in the country, Katlyn? To spend a quiet weekend away from school and work? To get back in touch with nature?"

Carol Banner's breezy attitude lost some of its air when she gazed at the glum face of her 15-year-old daughter. "Oh, Mom, this will be so boring," Katlyn griped. "I can't believe you dragged me out here to nowhere land. I could be with my friends right now, having a good time at the mall or hanging out at the square."

Carol pursed her lips. "Katlyn, you can make life pleasant for the two of us and enjoy the weekend or you can be miserable. I'm not going to let you spoil my fun."

"Fun? You call this fun?" whined Katlyn, sweeping her hand at the crowded campground. "We get to sleep on the ground next to strangers, walk through poison ivy and briar patches, and possibly get eaten by bears."

Carol tried to keep a grip on her patience. "Katlyn, we

sleep on air mattresses in a tent with a floor, we hike on the paths where there are no poisonous plants, and bears don't like the taste of humans—especially sourpusses. Come on, give it a try. Who knows, you might actually like it."

"Yeah, right," groused Katlyn, folding her arms.

"Take a deep breath and smell the air."

Katlyn gave a fake cough. "I think I smell the pig farm we passed down the road."

"Listen to the sounds of Mother Nature," said Carol. She couldn't have said it at a worst possible moment. As soon as the words tumbled out of her mouth, the blast from a passing train shattered the peace.

"What was that, Mom, the Mother Nature Express?" the moody teen asked sarcastically.

"Katlyn, enough," Carol snapped.

"I can't believe you picked a campground right near the railroad tracks. If the noise won't get us, the hoboes will."

"There are no hoboes anymore. Katlyn, you're not making this easy. I thought maybe with Dad and the boys gone for the weekend we could hike and talk. You know, girl stuff."

Katlyn rolled her eyes and said, "Oh, Mom, puh-*leeze*." But she quickly realized that her sarcasm had hurt her mother's feelings. *Maybe I pushed too far*, Katlyn thought. *She's just trying to be a mom. I guess it wouldn't hurt to be a little nicer.*

Katlyn put her arm around her mother's slumped shoulders. "Mom, I'm sorry. Really. I was out of line. I guess I'm still a little upset over my breakup with James. Come on, let's go for a hike. But are you sure we won't be hassled by any bears or hoboes?"

* * *

Mother and daughter enjoyed their stroll. The park trails wound through a hardwood forest in North Carolina's Piedmont, where a canopy of sweet gum, dogwood, and sourwood shaded ferns and wildflowers.

That night Katlyn tossed and turned in her sleeping bag, unable to get comfortable lying atop an air mattress. And her breakup with her boyfriend James still kept her up nights. It had been three weeks, but thoughts of James kept popping into her head. Her sleep wasn't helped any by the long noisy, rattling freight trains that barreled down the tracks twice just when she was about to doze off. The train tracks were only a few hundred yards from the campground, behind a thick stand of loblolly pine.

Mom couldn't have picked a worse spot to camp, Katlyn thought. *These trains are driving me nuts. I think I'll go for a little walk.* She put on her shoes, grabbed a flashlight, stepped out of the tent, and aimlessly followed a trail. *The moon looks awfully bright and pretty tonight, just like the night James and I started to go steady. Hey, stop thinking about James. It's over. He's crazy about Jenny now. I've got to get him out of my mind. Mom is right about one thing. There are other fish in the sea, but I don't know if I feel like —*

"Did you come out here to see the death and destruction?"

Katlyn let out a frightened shriek, dropping her flashlight.

A man in his sixties, tall as a post and thin as a rail, leaned on a cane as he limped out from the bushes and onto the trail. "Sorry, Miss, I didn't mean to scare you none."

"Stay away from me," Katlyn hissed. "I know karate." She immediately crouched into a defensive stance with her hands out in front of her body.

"Take it easy, Miss. I'm not looking for trouble. There'll be plenty soon enough. Just go on your way. I'm not going to bother you."

With one eye on the man, Katlyn stooped down, picked up the flashlight, and pointed it at him. The man wore a tattered blue-and-white striped engineer's cap and a frayed, light blue long-sleeved shirt under denim overalls soiled with oil and grease. Gray stubble sprouted from his bony face. His dark eyes were set back so deep under bushy gray eyebrows that at first Katlyn thought he didn't even have eyes. She shined her flashlight directly in his face, causing him to shield his eyes with his forearm. "Mind if you quit blinding me?"

"Sorry," she said, aiming the beam down. "Just stay where you are and don't take any steps toward me."

"It's good that you're wary of strangers. You shouldn't be out here alone."

"I'm not alone," she fibbed. "What do you mean there's going to be death and destruction?"

"Tragedy would be another word. Or calamity. Or maybe catastrophe."

"Why? What's going to happen?"

The man began hobbling down the path. "I think it best if you just get on back to wherever you came from."

"Are you a hobo?"

The old man leaned on his cane and laughed until he began to cough. "Hobo, huh? That's a good one. No, I'm not a hobo. In fact, I used to kick hoboes out of the railroad yard over in Charlotte. Yep, way back when hoboes would hop into empty freight cars and ride the rails. People like to think of hoboes as great philosophers and thinkers who were struck with wanderlust."

"Wanderlust?"

"An urge to wander or travel. But the truth is most hoboes were drunks and ne'er-do-wells, bums who didn't want to work or be a part of society." He pulled out a gold pocket watch and stared at it. "Darn eyesight isn't what it used to be. Would you be kind enough to shine your flashlight on my watch? Ah, much better, thank you. It's nearly 2 A.M. If you'll excuse me, I'd better mosey down to the tracks. I don't want to miss it."

"Miss what?"

"Number Nine."

"Is that a train?"

"Was a train, Miss. Emphasis on the *was*. By the way, my name is Cecil Jacobson." He tipped his cap and bowed his head.

"Hi, my name is—" Katlyn caught herself. "Never mind."

"You're a cautious young lady. That's fine. Caution is a good thing, but I don't think it would have helped ol' Number Nine. Sorry, Miss, but I've got to keep walking. As old as I am, it's going to take me a little while to get near the tracks. I've waited 50 years to see this."

Katlyn knew she should head straight back to the campground, but the old man had totally captured her interest. *I've got to find out what's going on,* she told herself. *He seems harmless. But I'll keep a safe distance from him. Besides I'm a brown belt in karate, so I'm not afraid of him.*

"Mr. Jacobson, what's going to happen?"

"If you want to know, you'll have to follow me. I can tell you on the way." He continued to limp down the path while Katlyn trailed several feet behind him.

"Exactly 50 years to this day, a woman was driving by here when she had a flat tire at about 2 A.M. While she was trying to fix it, she saw the light of a train. All of a sudden she heard the screeching and crashing sounds of metal and wood. She ran toward Bostian's Bridge, just over yonder, and saw smashed cars and bodies lying everywhere. People were screaming. She ran for help and came to my house, which is just over the ridge on this side of Third Creek and banged on our door. Must have been around 3 o'clock. Darn near scared me silly. I was 12 years old at the time. She was hysterical and begged my daddy to come see for himself. Since I was the oldest kid in our family, he let me go with him. We followed her back to Bostian's Bridge. We brought along a couple of lanterns. I was getting worked up about seeing all this death and destruction. But when we got to the scene there wasn't anything to see—least-wise, no train wreck. She kept babbling on that she saw the crash. I figured she was a nut case.

"But my daddy, he didn't get sore or anything. He calmed her down and said, 'Lady, you might have seen a crash even though there ain't one.' Now I'm thinking that maybe Daddy is touched in the head too. Then he took her back to our house.

"Daddy worked for the railroad, so he knew all about trains. He went into the desk drawer and pulled out an old newspaper clipping and he said, 'Yep, you just described the worst train wreck that ever happened in this state.' And then he showed the article to her. She read it and broke out wailing, 'That's exactly what I saw!'"

Cecil fumbled around in his pocket and took out a tattered clipping. "It's too dark to read, and I don't have my reading glasses, but it says basically that very early one morning, passenger train Number Nine left Salisbury for Asheville. Two miles (3 km) out, at Bostian's Bridge, the entire train ran off the bridge and fell 75 feet (22.5 m) into Third Creek. About 30 people were killed, and dozens more were injured. It was a terrible tragedy."

He handed the clipping to Katlyn. Shining her flashlight onto the article, she read: "APPALLING TRAGEDY!! The most horrible disaster in the history of railroading in North Carolina occurred early Thursday morning at Bostian's Bridge over Third Creek. The westbound passenger train, No. 9, was hurled from the top of the bridge . . ." She handed the article back to Cecil.

"Now here's where it gets interesting," he continued. "The train wreck happened at about 2:15 A.M. on August 27, 1891. The lady saw the same wreck at 2:15 A.M. on August 27, 1941—exactly 50 years later to the minute! When Daddy told her that, she plum swooned and fell right into my arms. It took a full five minutes for her to come around."

By now Cecil and Katlyn had reached the top of a ravine. In the moonlight a few hundred yards away, they saw a train trestle spanning a bold stream 75 feet (22.5 m) below them. "Ah, this looks like a perfect vantage point," said Cecil. Pointing to a span made of rock and brick, he added, "That there is Bostian's Bridge." Five arches, each about 40 feet (12 m) wide, held the bridge up over the steep ravine.

Cecil slowly ambled to a rock and sat down with a grunt. "People claim that the train was going too fast. But don't you believe it. The engineer on Number Nine was the best, safest motorman ever to open a throttle valve. I've been waiting a long time to prove to myself that he wasn't to blame. And now I'm only minutes away from finding out."

"What are you saying?" asked Katlyn, tossing her hands in the air. "That the train is going to crash again?"

"The lady saw the ghost of the Number Nine wreck exactly 50 years after the crash. It stands to reason that maybe it will do the same thing again after another 50 years have passed. Today is August 27, 1991, exactly 100 years since the big wreck. I tried to get my friends and family to come here, but they thought my train wasn't pulling a full tender, if you get my drift."

Why don't you get out of here right now, Katlyn? she told herself. *He's a crazy man, an old fool. Get back before Mom wakes up and freaks out because you're not there. This man is sitting here in the middle of the night waiting for a ghost train!*

"Do you have the time?" Cecil asked.

"It's 2:10."

"Should be coming along any second now."

"Well, I'd better get going," said Katlyn. She began walking back when, in the distance, she heard *chug-chug-chug*. With every passing second, it grew louder.

Cecil clapped his hands. "How about that? Right on time."

"But if what you say is true, how can you be so happy reliving a tragedy?"

"It's history. What's happened has happened. Nothing I can do will change it. I don't relish the idea of watching people die like this. But I need to know what caused the train to crash."

The engine's whistle pierced the night with a mournful wail. Then Katlyn saw a pinprick of a light that grew bigger and brighter as the train approached Bostian's Bridge.

In the moonlight the train chugged into view as it rounded the bend and headed for the bridge. A steam engine complete with cowcatcher belched white smoke that curled over the coal car and four other coaches.

This isn't a ghost train, Katlyn thought. *It's too real. He's making this whole story up. The train is probably a replica heading for an exhibition.*

"I thought so!" yelled Cecil. "The train is going only about 20 miles (32 km) an hour, plenty safe. He wasn't speeding! No siree!" He pounded his cane on the ground. "He was doing right!"

The train was clacking its way across the bridge when suddenly the last coach shook crazily and veered off the tracks. As the coach toppled on its side it yanked the entire train to a momentary halt. Then the coach plunged off the bridge. To the sickening sounds of twisting metal and snapping wood, it pulled the other cars, one by one, into the darkness of the gorge. A thundering roar bellowed up from the bottom as the cars piled on top of one another.

The force of the derailment had ripped the tracks and cross-ties cleanly off the bridge. Rail, twisted like spaghetti, rained down upon the rubble.

It took only a few seconds for the train to be swept to its doom. Yet to Katlyn the horrifying scene played out in agonizing slow motion. Only after the entire train had ended up in a heap at the bottom of the gorge did she realize that she had been holding her breath. Katlyn sucked in air and then let it out with an ear-shattering scream.

"Now I know what happened!" cried out Cecil. "The ends of the ties at the approach to the bridge must have been rotten. As the last car passed over it, the ties gave way and the rails spread, causing the car to fall and drag the others with it."

"Who cares how it happened?" Katlyn barked. "These people need help!"

Screams of agony and terror and cries for help echoed off the sides of the gorge. Horror-stricken, Katlyn dashed toward the wreck. "Miss, don't go down there!" ordered Cecil. "You don't understand. What you're seeing is a different kind of real. Come back! You could get hurt."

But Katlyn didn't listen to him. To her this was no ghost train. *You can see through ghosts,* Katlyn thought. But the sickening sights and sounds were much too real. She saw metal and wood and human beings.

Katlyn scrambled down the steep embankment. But

she couldn't get close enough to the victims because they were on the other side of the fast-moving stream. Dazed men and women frantically tried to squeeze out of smashed windows and gashes in the coaches while others tried to pull victims to safety. Passengers who had crawled out waded to the bank. But now another danger loomed. The huge pile of debris had completely dammed up the stream, which already had been swollen from summer rains. The rising water was entering the coaches.

In the midst of the cries and groans an enormous sense of grief and helplessness overcame Katlyn. *I can't sit here and watch this. I must get help.* Katlyn climbed back up the embankment to the rock where she had last seen Cecil. But he was gone.

She scurried blindly through the woods back to the camp, stumbling and falling several times, skinning her knees and elbows. Bursting into the tent, Katlyn shouted, "Mom! Mom! We need to get to a phone to call 911! I saw a terrible train wreck. Bodies everywhere! People hurt!"

"We'll drive to the nearest house and call from there," said Carol, throwing on her clothes. She grabbed her keys, and the two raced to the car. They roared out of the campground and sped off down a dirt road until they arrived at a small two-story, tin-roofed frame house.

Katlyn leaped out, bounded up the steps, and pounded on the front door. "Please open up! This is an emergency!" After a minute the porch light went on. A gray-haired woman in a ratty robe peered out from behind the door and asked, "What is it?"

"There's been a terrible train wreck!" shouted Katlyn.

"We need to use your phone to call 911!"

Katlyn started to walk past the woman, but the elderly woman threw out her arm and blocked her. "What kind of wreck?"

"A steam engine and several cars fell off the bridge and down the gorge. Please, we're wasting precious time. Where's your phone?"

"So he was right after all, the poor dear." The woman shook her head, shuffled over to a chair, sat down, and began to cry. Meanwhile, Katlyn searched for the phone. "Where is the phone?" she demanded.

"Young lady, calm down," said the woman. "You don't need the phone. There was no train wreck tonight."

"But I saw it with my own eyes!"

"What you saw were ghostly images of a terrible event, an event that happened 100 years ago."

Katlyn sank into the nearest chair. "That's what Cecil told me."

The woman gasped. "You saw Cecil? When?"

"Just a short while ago. I met him on a path near the bridge. He told me all about the accident and how a woman saw it happen 50 years later."

"Wait a minute," snarled the woman. "Are you playing some cruel joke on me?"

Carol, who had followed Katlyn into the house, marched up to the woman and declared, "Ma'am, my daughter doesn't lie. Look at her. She's scared out of her wits. Why would you doubt her?"

"Because Cecil is my husband...my *dead* husband. He died two weeks ago!"

Katlyn's mouth dropped open. "There must be some mistake. The man was in his sixties, tall and skinny and wearing an engineer's cap and coveralls."

"Did he walk with a cane?"

Katlyn nodded.

"That's Cecil!"

Now it was Katlyn's turn to cry. "I don't understand. You tell me I saw a train crash that happened 100 years ago and that all those people screaming and crying were ghosts. And then you tell me that the person I saw it with was a ghost too."

"Cecil was absolutely convinced that the wreck of Number Nine would be relived on its 100th anniversary. His friends and family laughed at him. But he didn't mind. He was determined to see it, just like that woman did 50 years ago. Unfortunately Cecil got very sick. Cancer. He knew he was dying. But he wanted to live long enough to see that crash." Her voice choked up again. "He just couldn't quite make it."

"But he did make it," said Katlyn. "He saw the crash."

"Mrs. Jacobson," asked Carol, "why did Cecil care so much about this wreck?"

"As a boy Cecil adored his grandfather, Chester Jacobson. Chester was the engineer of Number Nine, and he was accused of causing the wreck by traveling too fast. He died in the crash, so he couldn't defend himself. From then on the blame that blotted Chester's name gnawed at Cecil. He never believed his grandfather was at fault."

"Well, he was right," said Katlyn. "Cecil saw the crash with his own eyes. I heard him say the train was going at a safe speed and that rotten ties were to blame for the wreck."

Mrs. Jacobson clasped her hands. "Thank goodness. Cecil no longer will be haunted by doubt. Now he knows the truth."

THE GHOSTS OF MOOREHAVEN BRIDGE

B. J. Moore and his new friend Tiki Fuller galloped their horses through the Mississippi lowlands on a muggy summer afternoon. For the two teens and their steeds, it was the first day of a weekend camping trip on land owned by the Moore family for over 150 years.

B. J. and Tiki had struck up a fast friendship although they came from worlds apart. Born into wealth, B. J. lived in a beautiful colonial brick mansion on a sprawling estate, while Tiki lived in a modest house on a small horse farm. B. J. was white and Tiki was African-American. But the two 14-year-olds were alike in many ways. Both were good athletes and students who loved horses. Both came from families whose roots in Mississippi went back to the early 1800s.

When they went camping the boys had no idea that their bloodlines would lead them into the creepy world of the beyond.

B. J. and Tiki slowed their horses to a trot as they reached the old stone Moorehaven Bridge, which spanned a lazy river. The wood planks on the surface of the bridge clattered under the horses' hooves. Suddenly, Tiki's horse, Apache, reared up.

"Settle down, Apache," ordered Tiki as he leaned forward to keep from falling off. Apache whinnied, backed up, and then reared again. "I don't know what's wrong with her, B. J. She never acts this way."

Tiki pulled on the reins and gave Apache a kick. "Easy, girl, easy." Finally, he calmed her down and guided her to the other side.

"I think she got spooked by the bridge," said B. J.

"She's crossed bridges before."

"Not one like this," B. J. said. "The Moorehaven Bridge is haunted. Over the years people have heard strange moans and other sounds. They say it's been happening ever since the 1800s. I think it has to do with the ghost of a murder victim."

"Aw, I don't believe in ghosts."

"It looks like Apache does," B. J. chuckled.

They decided to pitch their tent in a clearing a few hundred yards from the bridge.

Later that afternoon the boys rode past the remains of an old shack about a half mile (792 m) from the bridge. The rusted tin roof had caved in on one side, and the windows and front door were missing. Holes from bullets and insects riddled the rotted wood walls. The crumbling stone chimney leaned so far over, it looked ready to topple at any minute.

"What was that?" asked Tiki.

"I'm not sure. An old shanty from the plantation days, I guess."

Unexplainably, Tiki felt drawn to the shack. He got off his horse and walked around the shanty. It was covered by kudzu, a fast-growing leafy weed, and surrounded by tall grass. He peered inside and for a moment a distressing vision entered his mind: A lean, sweaty black man lying on his stomach on a crude handmade wooden cot in the corner; his back and side bleeding with long, slashing cuts, the kind made from a whip; a woman sobbing next to him, dipping a bloodied cloth into water and dabbing it on his wounds.

"Look out, Tiki," warned B. J. "Yellow jackets are right next to you, and they don't look very friendly."

Tiki's vision disappeared as a squadron of angry hornets buzzed around his head. He scrambled away from the shack and hopped on his horse.

"See anything in there, Tiki?"

"Yes and no. I mean, there's nothing inside, but I had the strangest vision. It was like I could almost see a slave being treated for whip lashes on his back."

Tiki didn't talk much for the next ten minutes. His mind kept drifting to the vision in the shack. He had a feeling it meant something, but he didn't know what. He would soon learn its chilling significance.

After exploring the countryside they headed their horses back to the campsite. The horses were trotting across the Moorehaven Bridge when a strange breeze rose from the river—but it swirled around only Tiki and Apache. The sudden gust of cold wind chilled Tiki's neck.

Apache's ears twitched forward, a sure sign she was frightened. Her eyes grew wide and she began to neigh.

To his utter surprise Tiki felt someone jump right behind him on the horse and lean on his back. He turned around and gulped in astonishment—no one was there. Just then a pair of invisible hands forcefully gripped his shoulders, sending icy waves of fear penetrating to his bones.

Before Tiki could react, Apache reared up, nearly tossing him off the bridge and into the river. The horse let out another terrified neigh and began bucking like a bronco, trying to throw everyone off her back. But Tiki held on.

Apache continued to rear and kick, paying no heed to the cries from her rider. Suddenly Tiki heard groans coming from beneath the bridge. It sounded like the pain-wracked sounds of a dying man. He muttered a few words, but Tiki could make out only one. It sounded like "joad."

Suddenly Apache sprinted across the bridge. When they reached the other side, the frightful moans stopped. But the invisible hitchhiker still held onto Tiki as Apache galloped uncontrollably, like the leader of a stampede. She moved much too swiftly for Tiki to jump off. The faster Apache ran, the tighter the hands gripped the teen's shoulders. With his left hand grasped tightly around the reins, Tiki used his right hand to reach around his back, trying to push the rider off. But it was useless. The invisible rider wouldn't let go.

After a frantic half-mile (792 m) gallop, Tiki finally regained control of Apache. As the horse slowed down, the mysterious hands relaxed their grasp on Tiki's shoulders. Seconds later the boy sensed that the unseen hitchhiker had jumped off.

Tiki brought his trembling, snorting horse to a halt. They were in front of the old shack he had seen hours earlier.

"Tiki, is everything okay?" asked B. J. as he galloped up on his bounding horse, Dandy. "Man, I couldn't keep up with you. What's going on?"

"I—I don't know," Tiki replied. "I was going across the bridge when I heard strange moaning. It sounded like a man was dying."

"Yeah, I heard it too. Dandy got real skittish and reared up, but nothing like what Apache did. I told you the bridge was haunted."

Tiki jumped off Apache, whose shoulders and flanks were wet with foam and sweat. He began walking her, hoping to calm her—and himself. "B. J., that's not all. I know this is going to sound bizarre, but I felt someone hop on the back of Apache. He was invisible. I felt ice-cold hands around my shoulders, and Apache went wild. We ended up here in front of this shack, and that's where the rider jumped off. I'm not making this stuff up. I was scared, and so was Apache."

"Tiki, let's go back to our camp. It's getting dark."

"Okay, but first let me look inside this shack again." He snooped around, hoping to find a clue to the strange ordeal he had experienced. He came away without finding anything or seeing any vision like the earlier one.

"Do you want to head home instead?" asked B. J.

Tiki glared at him and snapped, "I'm not afraid, okay? I'm no baby."

When they returned to their camp, they made dinner, went hunting for bullfrogs, and then sat around their small, flickering fire.

"Tiki, I've got something to tell you," said B. J. "It's about the bridge and the shack. I wasn't kidding when I told you the bridge was haunted. I know more about it than I've let on. My family has told me who the moaning ghost is. It's not a pleasant story. In fact, it's pretty awful. It goes way back to the 1840s. This was a plantation back then, and my ancestors owned a lot of slaves, including one named Joad. He once lived in that shack we saw today."

"Joad? I heard the moaning voice on the bridge say that name. B. J., do you think it was his ghost who was groaning?"

"No, but you might have seen his ghost in the shack. In fact, he's responsible for the moaning ghost."

"Why didn't you tell me about Joad?"

"I guess I was afraid of how you would react knowing that my ancestors owned slaves. We're not like that, Tiki."

"Hey, man, that was a long time ago. I can't blame you or your family today for what happened in the last century. I know you and your folks are cool. So what gives? What's the story about the bridge?"

"The land was divided by the Moore family so that four brothers each had five hundred acres. All of the brothers, including my great-great-great-grandfather Benedict, had slaves working on the plantations. Three of the brothers treated their slaves well. But the fourth, Hale, was cruel. He wasn't respected by the other brothers. He would walk around with a bullwhip and use it on any slave he thought looked at him the wrong way."

As the bullfrogs croaked in the night, B. J. told about one of the worst, and spookiest, chapters in the Moore family history.

Among Hale Moore's slaves was a middle-aged man named Joad, who had been working on the plantation since he was ten years old when he and his mother were sold to Hale. Joad got off on the wrong foot when Hale caught him fishing in the river without permission. He was trying to get extra food for his mother and had caught several good-sized fish. But Hale demanded that Joad turn the catch over to him. Rather than give it to his master, Joad "accidentally" dropped his catch into the water. Hale was so enraged he shoved Joad into the swirling water. The boy didn't know how to swim, but he managed to reach the safety of the bank, coughing and sputtering. From then on, he was a marked man. At every opportunity, Hale made life miserable for Joad. The master whipped him and punished him for the slightest offense.

One day, Hale, clutching his bullwhip, stood over a group of slaves who were tending the fields. No matter how hard Joad worked, it wasn't good enough for Hale. When Joad stopped for a moment's rest, Hale thundered, "I didn't tell you to stop!" Then he raised his whip and snapped its vicious tail. It lashed across Joad's scarred, bare back.

Hours later Joad was hoeing by the Moorehaven Bridge away from the others. He had reached the point where anything, even death, would be better than suffering one more lash from Hale's whip. The salt from his sweat burned his wounded back. Hurting and hot in the stifling afternoon heat, Joad looked longingly at the cool, clear river. He knew if he could just sit down in the water for only a moment, it would soothe his wound and refresh his body.

Joad looked around for Hale and didn't see him. So the

slave dropped his hoe and slid quietly into the water. He didn't dare make a splash out of fear that the noise would alert Hale. Joad knew he should stay in the river for only a second so he wouldn't get caught. But once in the refreshing water, he couldn't make himself get out. No, it was worth the risk to feel the rush of cool water caressing his weary back, washing away the sweat, dirt, and blood. He closed his eyes and allowed himself a minute to dream of a day when he'd have the freedom to jump into any river he wanted for as long as he wanted.

Suddenly Hale Moore's bellowing voice jolted the day-dreaming slave back to harsh reality. "You slacker! You swine!" The furious master lashed out with the whip as Joad scrambled to the bank. The whip sliced across Joad's side from his lower back to the front of his ribs.

Yelping in pain, Joad picked up his hoe and held it horizontally in front of his body, trying to ward off the next attack. When Hale again lashed his whip, it wrapped around Joad's hoe. Enraged, Hale yanked on the whip and jerked the hoe out of Joad's hands. But in doing so, Hale lost his balance. He stumbled backwards, striking his head hard against a pointed rock. Hale moaned and groaned, holding the back of his head. "Joad!" he hissed. "Joad!" Hale staggered to his feet and then collapsed, falling face-first into the river.

Without thinking, Joad rushed into the water and pulled Hale to shore. He slapped his unconscious master in an attempt to revive him. Joad hit him again and again, and without realizing it, his blows became stronger and stronger as years of pent-up rage rose to the surface.

Finally, Joad stopped and put his ear to Hale's chest. There was no heartbeat. His master was dead.

Joad panicked. No one would believe the truth, he feared. If they found Hale they would see he had been beaten. They would conclude that Joad had attacked his master in retaliation for the whipping he had received earlier in the day. Joad knew he had to do something, and fast.

The slave dragged Hale under the bridge. He hurriedly hollowed out a grave in the damp earth and placed his master's body, and whip, inside. Then he covered up the hole just as Tucker, an older slave who was exercising Mrs. Hale's horse, approached the bridge. Meanwhile, off in the distance, Joad heard the sound of thundering hooves. He feared they were the galloping horses of the other Moore brothers. He had to get out of there.

As Tucker guided the trotting horse across the bridge, Joad hopped on its back, gripped Tucker's shoulders, and ordered him to head out. They sped over to Joad's house, where his wife tended to his wounds.

When Hale failed to show up for dinner, family members went looking for him. One of the Moore brothers, aware of the whipping earlier that day, questioned Joad. But the slave claimed he didn't know his master's whereabouts. A search party scoured the land for days without success.

Several years after Hale's disappearance, people began sharing accounts of bizarre incidents on Moorehaven Bridge. Slaves and family members reported hearing moaning and the cracking sound of a whip as they approached the bridge. On certain nights, if someone with a torch began walking across the bridge, the light would mysteriously go out, only to blaze once more when the bearer had crossed to the other side. Horses that had cantered across the bridge dozens of times before suddenly would whinny and refuse to cross.

No one knew why until Benedict Moore made a grim discovery many years later.

Benedict was crossing the bridge when his horse reared. As he was getting his steed under control he heard a moan and a man's gasping voice mumbling a word that sounded like "joad." Benedict got off his horse and looked under the bridge. Recent heavy rains had caused the river to rise, tearing into the bank and washing away rocks and layers of dirt. Noticing an object sticking out of the bank, Benedict tugged on it and pulled out a bullwhip. He instantly recognized it as his missing brother's. Digging further, he found a skull and other bones.

Although he couldn't prove it, Benedict believed they were Hale's remains. Recalling the moaning and the sound like "joad" he had heard minutes earlier, Benedict decided to pay Joad a visit. Joad, who had been set free at the end of the Civil War, had remained on the land to work a few acres as a sharecropper. But his hard life had taken its toll. Old and frail, Joad lay on his deathbed when Benedict arrived.

As soon as Joad saw Benedict holding the whip in his hand, the former slave broke down and admitted what had happened on that fateful day. "It was an accident and that's the truth," he said. "I was afraid that if I came forward, no one would believe me, and I would be killed and my family harmed. I couldn't take that chance. As much as I wanted to tell you, I couldn't bring myself to do it. I've had to live with the burden of knowing about Master Hale's death all these years. I'm an old man, now. I'm a free man—free from everything but guilt. Do what you want with me."

Benedict knew that Joad had suffered enough, first because of Hale and then from his own conscience. Taking Joad at his word, Benedict assured him that no further harm would come to him. It wouldn't matter anyway. Benedict was convinced that Joad wouldn't survive the night.

Although Benedict had had little respect for Hale, he still felt sad that the remains he found were those of his brother. Only after Benedict learned the truth did he understand why the bridge was haunted. The moans and the uttering of Joad's name came from the ghost of Hale Moore.

Early the next morning Benedict was riding his horse when he noticed the outstretched body of a man lying on his stomach at one end of the bridge. He quickly dismounted, ran to the body, and turned it over. To his shock, he saw that it was Joad, dead.

"To this day," B. J. told Tiki, "no one knows how an old man could have risen from his deathbed and traveled a half mile (792 m) from his cabin before collapsing at the bridge. And no one knows why he did it either."

"Maybe he wanted to make peace," said Tiki, picking up a stick and stirring the glowing embers of the campfire. He stared at the flames, not speaking for a long time.

"What are you thinking about, Tiki?"

"The invisible hitchhiker. You don't suppose it was Joad's ghost, do you? I mean, I felt this unseen person all the way to Joad's shack, and then he jumped off. What about when I looked inside the shack? I had this vision of a black man being treated for slash marks. And that was before I knew anything about this. It had to be Joad."

"Oh, wow, you could be right."

"B. J., has anyone ever mentioned an invisible hitchhiker?"

"Never."

"Why did it happen to me?"

The answer would come soon enough.

That night the boys were sleeping in their tent when their horses began to neigh and paw at the ground. Tiki woke up first and peeked out of the flap. Thunder rumbled in the distance, so he assumed the horses were sensing a storm. He walked over to the animals and talked softly, trying to comfort them.

Then he headed back toward the tent, when a loud crack startled him. At first he thought it was caused by lightning. But there were no flashes in the sky. He continued walking.

WHIT...CRACK...WHIT...CRACK!

Tiki wheeled around. On the other side of the smoldering campfire stood a chubby man in a tan cowboy hat, open shirt, brown pants, and boots. His angry eyes glowed as red as the embers. His lips curled in a sneer as he raised his whip and expertly snapped it.

WHIT...CRACK...WHIT...CRACK!

"I have come for my revenge!" he growled.

"What are you talking about?" Tiki gulped, flinching at the loud crack.

The man snapped his whip again, causing the horses to jerk their heads and whinny with alarm.

"Get away from me," cried Tiki.

The man ignored him and moved closer, stunning the frightened teen even more: The man didn't walk around the campfire, he seemed to float right over it!

Tiki shook his head, dumfounded. All he knew for sure was that this was no vision.

"You don't give me orders!" hissed the man. "I give you orders! Ten lashes! I should have finished you off when I had the chance!"

The man advanced steadily toward Tiki, who stood still, not knowing what to do. As crazy as it sounded, Tiki's first thought was that he was staring at a ghost.

"Are you Hale Moore?" the boy asked.

"Have you lost your mind? Of course I am! Master Hale Moore! Did you think you could get away with your crime?"

"What crime?"

"Murder!"

He's a ghost! Tiki told himself. *And he thinks I'm Joad! Now what do I do?* Mustering up his courage, Tiki fired back, "It wasn't murder. It was an accident. You brought it on yourself. You were heartless and cruel—and it cost you your life." *Oh, boy, now I've really got him mad.*

Raging in anger, the ghost bobbed closer, raised his arm, cocked his wrist, and let fly the whip. It took only a second, but to Tiki it seemed to happen in slow motion. The whip curled in the air like a coiled snake and then lashed straight at the terrified teen. He held up his hands as a shield, turned his head away, and crouched low. "Nooooo!" he cried out.

"Tiki! Tiki!" yelled B. J., storming out of the tent. "What's wrong?"

Tiki cautiously came out of his crouch and looked

around. He had not been harmed. The ghost was gone. The horses had quieted. Relieved yet shaky, Tiki staggered over to a log and sat down. "B. J., I just saw the ghost of Hale Moore!"

"He was here?"

"Yes, he thought I was Joad. He tried to whip me, but he disappeared when you came out of the tent."

"Tiki, I don't know what to say."

"B. J., I don't know what to think."

At the Moore mansion Tiki told his incredible story to his parents and B. J.'s. "Why was Hale's ghost picking on me? And why did Joad hitch a ride with me?"

"Wait here," said B. J.'s father. He went into another room and returned with an old leather-bound log book. He flipped through the yellowed pages. "This was a list of the sharecroppers who lived here on the plantation after the Civil War. Here it is: 'Joad Brown. Given four acres for cotton. Died in 1870.'"

"Joad Brown?" gasped Tiki's mother, leaping to her feet. "My great-great-grandfather was named Joad Brown. He was a sharecropper in this area back then. It has to be the same man!"

"That explains everything," B. J.'s dad exclaimed. "Hale and Joad both died on the bridge. Their ghosts have been tormented ever since. The ghosts appeared because this was the first time that their blood relatives were on the bridge at the same time. Joad's ghost hitched a ride with Tiki, reliving the moment of his getaway after burying Hale. And then Hale's ghost tried to seek vengeance through Tiki."

"It's sad," Tiki said, "that after all these years, they still aren't at rest."

"And what's worse," added B. J., "it looks like they never will be."

THE WOOD-GIVERS

Ever since the divorce became official, 13-year-old Lexi Phelan and her 12-year-old sister Demi had been trying to get their mother, Sandy, to take them on a weekend camping trip in the Colorado Rockies.

"It will be good for you, Mom," said Lexi. "It will give you a chance to bond with your two perfect daughters."

Demi laughed in her distinct, high-pitched way and added, "Yeah, Mom, we'll leave here as city girls and return as new live-by-our-wits wilderness women."

"Oh, I don't know," said Sandy, running her fingers through her curly blond hair. "It's been so long since we last camped. When was that? Three or four years ago? And that turned into disaster when your dad and I —"

"Stop it, Mom," snapped Lexi, her hazel eyes flashing. "No more talk about Dad. He left us. He's out of our life. It's just the three of us now." Then, turning off her hurt and anger, she winked and cooed, "Come on, it will be good for you—and for us." Lexi playfully tugged on her mother's arm and pleaded, "Puh-leez?"

Demi tugged Sandy's other arm. "We'll be totally alone. We'll return with a new sense of independence."

"What do you mean?" asked Sandy.

"Back-country camping," Demi replied. "We'll carry all our supplies to a really remote site where no one else is around. Just Mother Nature. It will be our great adventure!"

Added Lexi, "One we'll always cherish."

And one they would never forget.

Fluffy popcorn clouds skittered across the pale blue sky, playing hide-and-seek with the September sun. The rays filtered through the towering pines, casting a soft glow on the forest floor. The breeze blew gently as they unloaded their car at the staging area.

"Oh, what a glorious day!" declared Sandy, throwing her arms up in happiness. "I feel so good!"

"That's the spirit, Mom!" chirped Lexi, giving her mother a big hug.

"The weather report said it should be a pretty good weekend," Sandy said. "A cold front is coming this way, but it shouldn't arrive until we're back home."

When loaded up, each carried about 30 pounds (13.6 kg) of supplies on her back. Sandy smiled to herself when she saw her daughters hauling so much gear. From behind they looked like headless backpacks with arms and legs. Fortunately, the girls were athletic and in excellent shape. Although more slender, their mother worked out regularly at a local gym and felt confident she could carry her load.

"Onward and upward—in more ways than one!" shouted Sandy.

Singing a rousing version of "I Am Woman," the trio headed out along a gently sloping trail that led them up past 12,000 feet (3,600 m) elevation. As the path climbed higher the woods changed from ponderosa pine to Douglas fir. Maples, cottonwoods, and aspens added splashes of yellows and reds to the otherwise deep green forest.

"This is so cool," Lexi squealed. "I can't believe we're doing this."

"Believe it!" declared Demi. "We're the wilderness women!"

After hiking for six miles (9.6 km), the now-weary family reached a primitive campsite by a mountain stream, where they pitched their tent and collected firewood.

Demi was the first to notice the strange snickering. "Did you hear that?" she asked Lexi. "It sounds like little kids giggling." The two girls stood still and listened. "There it is again."

Haa-haa, hee-hee, tee-hee.

"You're right," Lexi said. Her shoulders drooped in disappointment. "What a bummer. We walk for miles to get away from everyone only to find out we're not alone."

"Come on, let's go see. I think it's coming from over there," Demi said, pointing to a clump of larch trees.

Every 30 seconds the girls stopped in their tracks and listened for the snickers. By now the sun had dropped behind the mountain ridge, turning the air chillier.

Haa-haa, hee-hee, tee-hee.

"It's weird," Lexi said. "Every time we seem to be

getting closer to the giggling, it seems to come from another direction."

"Do you think the kids are playing games with us?"

"Could be. If so, they're making fools out of us."

"Come on, Lexi, let's get back to camp. Mom will be worried about —"

"Girls! Girls! Where are you?"

"See?" said Demi, poking her sister with an elbow. "What did I tell you?"

Demi and Lexi laughed as they scurried back to the camp. As the hours passed, the wind picked up and the trees swayed with more authority. And then the Phelans heard the giggling again.

"Darn those kids," complained Demi.

"Sure wrecks the mood," Lexi grumbled.

"Well," commented Sandy, "I guess we can't have the wilderness all to ourselves. I wonder where they're camping. You'd think we would have seen a flashlight or lantern or a fire coming from their camp."

Haa-haa, hee-hee, tee-hee.

"Now it's coming from over there," Demi said, pointing in front of them.

"No, it's coming from behind us," declared Lexi. "It's getting louder. They must be close."

"Girls, just ignore them."

"No, Mom, I want to find them," Lexi pouted. "They're lousing things up. It's not right." She picked up a flashlight but didn't turn it on. Then she walked off in the direction she last had heard the tittering. When Lexi disappeared into the darkness, where the flames no longer cast their glow, she stood still. She waited for telltale signs of the kids, their sniggering or the crunch of their feet as they walked over the pine-needle-covered ground.

The snickering returned, louder now but different. It sounded like surround-sound stereo, coming from all directions, and echoed as if the gigglers were in a chamber. Seconds later it stopped.

After several minutes of hearing nothing but the branches creaking in the stiff breeze, Lexi felt an unexplained wave of sadness. She pulled her jacket tight around her neck.

Now why do I feel so sad? she thought. *We've been in such an up mood all day. Must be because we're not alone. Darn, those kids! But, no, that's not it. This sadness seems deeper. Maybe it has to do with Dad deserting us. I don't know. This giggling has got me upset.*

Lexi joined Demi and her mother in the tent, where they crawled into their sleeping bags. She had a tough time falling asleep. Every time she tossed and turned, her air mattress squeaked.

"Lexi," Demi whispered in annoyance. "Will you stay still. With Mom snoring, it's hard enough to get to sleep without your air mattress making all that noise."

"I can't help it, Demi. I feel real down. I wish I could put my finger on it. That giggling makes me sad."

"Why would giggling make you sad? Giggling is a happy sound."

"It doesn't make sense, does it?"

Haa-haa, hee-hee, tee-hee.

"Lexi, did you hear that?"

"Yes. It was right outside our tent."

Armed with her flashlight, Lexi whipped open the flap of their tent. The beam scanned across the campsite. Meanwhile, Demi slipped out and searched behind the tent with another flashlight.

"See anything?" Lexi asked.

"Nothing. What about you?"

"Zip. And I didn't hear anyone walking away. With all the leaves and pine needles around here, we would have heard someone running away. Demi, is it my imagination or did the giggling seemed to echo and come from all directions?"

"It wasn't your imagination," said Demi.

"It was almost—I don't know if I should say this—ghostlike."

"Lexi, you've been reading too many ghost stories."

"Demi, promise me you won't say anything to Mom about me mentioning ghosts, okay? She'll think I'm nuts."

"What's the big deal? She already knows you are."

The next morning gray clouds galloped across the sky, whipped by a brisk breeze. The girls and their mother boiled water for a breakfast of cream of wheat and tea. Over the campfire they toasted bagels and slathered them with apple butter. Then they left their tent and campsite intact and set out for a day-long hike to Lake Piper and back.

No one talked about the giggling they had heard the night before, enjoying the illusion that they were out in the wilderness alone. After two hours of walking along a ridge they reached the top of a rocky cliff.

"Wow, what a view," Lexi marveled.

"It's gorgeous," added Demi. She glanced at her mother and noticed tears welling up in Sandy's eyes.

"Mom, what's wrong?"

"Oh, nothing," replied Sandy, quickly wiping her eyes with the back of her hand. "I have something in my eyes."

"Mom, come clean," said Lexi. "What's up?"

Sandy plopped down and sighed. "When your father and I were dating, we once hiked to this spot. It was the first time he told me he loved me. I just melted in his arms, and we sat that way for hours. There was no one else in the whole world then, just the two of us. Time stood still. We talked about the future and how we were meant to be together. It was one of those magical days." She shook her head and forced a sad smile. "It's strange how things don't end up the way you think they will."

"Mom," asked Demi, "why did Daddy desert us? One day he's our warm, caring father, and the next day he just walks out of our lives. It's been two years since he left, and he's never once called or sent a card or anything."

"As far as I'm concerned, we have no father," Lexi snapped, spitting out each word with anger. "He's out of our lives for good."

"Girls, please. I'm sorry I brought him up. Look, we agreed to make this a fun trip. Remember, we're the wilderness women! Let's go!"

The sisters gave their mother a hug before continuing their march toward Lake Piper.

They hadn't walked more than a few hundred yards when they heard a little girl weeping. "It's coming from over there," said Demi, pointing to a large house-sized boulder off the path. "Let's go." They rushed over to the boulder but found no one. Still, they could hear the girl crying.

"Hello!" shouted Sandy. "Hello! Where are you?" The

crying stopped. "Can we help you? We heard you crying. Please tell us where you are."

"Maybe she's lost," Demi said.

The crying began again, but farther into the woods. "Let's go after her," Lexi suggested. "Maybe she's frightened and doesn't know where to go."

For the next hour the trio trudged through the pathless underbrush following the sounds of the crying girl and yelling out to her. They weaved to the north and west, and turned east before doubling back to the west. And then the crying stopped.

After several minutes of silence the girls looked at Sandy. "Uh, Mom, do you have any clue where we are?" asked Demi.

"Oh, dear," said Sandy, "not really." She pulled out her compass. "In all the excitement of trying to find the little girl, I didn't pay attention to our direction. I don't know where we are or how to get back to the trail." She turned around in a circle, looking at the nearby ridges, hoping to see a familiar landmark. "Everything looks the same. Oh, why didn't I look at the compass earlier?" She gnawed on her lip and then pointed to the east. "I think we should go in that direction."

By now thick, low clouds had blanketed the higher ridges. The wind shifted, blowing a blast of cold air. The temperature had dropped by 20 degrees in less than an hour. Snow flurries fluttered and soon the heavy clouds opened up, dumping wet, thick snow. The Phelan women were not equipped for cold and snow. They had rain gear, which they put on over their clothes to stay dry. But it did little to keep them warm.

"We've got to get back before this snow gets any worse," Sandy said.

But the swirling snow made the visibility so bad that they couldn't see more than 100 feet (30 m) in front of them. "I'm getting cold," complained Lexi.

"And I'm getting scared," Demi whimpered.

"Girls, don't panic. Let's keep walking. We're bound to hit the trail."

Lexi clutched her mother's arm. "Mom, listen. I think I hear someone moaning."

"Do you think it's that little girl?" Demi asked.

"Could be," said Lexi. "But it sounds more like the groans of an older girl."

"Whoever it is, we must look for her," said Sandy. "It's obvious she's hurt."

"We tried looking for a girl and look where it got us," said Lexi. "We're lost in a snowstorm that's rapidly turning into a blizzard."

"Girls, we can't leave this person alone, especially in this weather. I can hardly see." The wind whipped the snow sideways, clinging to every branch, bush, and rock, stinging the girls' bare faces as they continued their futile search.

Above the now-shrieking wind, they heard a new sound, a whistling. "It sounds like someone calling out to us," said Demi, her teeth chattering with cold. "Let's follow it. We have nothing to lose."

"Except maybe our lives," Lexi murmured, shivering.

Through the ever-thickening snow, the trio trudged in single file, blindly following an unseen whistler. Often they had to stop and strain to hear the whistle, which changed directions while leading them through the forest. A half hour later, just as they reached a clearing, the whistling stopped.

"Look, Mom, a cabin!" Lexi shouted. Through the pelting snow they saw a small log cabin fronted by a rickety porch that barely held up a sagging roof.

"The whistler led us to shelter!" exclaimed Sandy.

They plodded through the snow and onto the porch, where they pounded on the door. When they didn't get an answer, they peered through the dirty windows. The dark cabin was empty except for a broken wooden chair lying in a corner. The walls and stone fireplace were barren.

"It's abandoned," yelled Sandy over the wind.

They tried opening the door but it wouldn't budge. Neither would the windows.

"They seem nailed shut," Lexi said in desperation. "Should we break a window?"

"Desperate situations call for desperate measures," replied Sandy, feeling around in the snow for a rock, her hand turning numb with cold.

"Mom, Lexi, look! The door is open!"

"How did that happen? We tried it just a minute ago."

"Who cares? Let's go!" They hurried inside and slammed the door closed.

"Thank goodness the whistler led us to this cabin," Sandy said with relief.

Lexi stared out the window. "It's strange that we never saw anyone. In this snow, you'd think there would be footprints. But there aren't any."

"The wind and falling snow might have covered them up," said Demi.

"Then how come ours are still visible?" Lexi asked.

"Forget about it," said Demi. "We're safe here. Let's hope this storm ends soon."

But the storm didn't let up. In fact, it turned worse, much worse. The Rockies had been hit with a freak fall blizzard, plunging temperatures more than 50 degrees in less than 12 hours. Inch after inch, the swirling snow piled up into drifts that soon reached the windows.

Meanwhile, mother and daughters huddled together on the dirt floor, shivering. Under their rain gear, Lexi wore shorts and a sweatshirt; Demi had jeans and a cotton shirt, while Sandy wore a T-shirt, vest, and jeans. It was hardly enough to ward off the increasingly cold temperatures.

"I'm freezing," said Demi. "We have a fireplace but no firewood."

Sandy picked up the broken chair and slammed it against the wall, breaking it into several pieces. She tossed them into the fireplace along with some candy wrappers and napkins from their backpacks, and taking a pack of matches out of her pocket, she lit a small fire. They warmed their hands. Without saying anything, they knew the fire wouldn't last long. And no one wanted to think what would happen to them if the temperature kept dipping and the snow kept piling up.

"Well, at least we have food, and we can melt snow for water," said Sandy.

"What good is food and water if we freeze to death?" Demi cried.

Sandy worried that she and the girls would suffer from hypothermia. When body temperature falls below 95 degrees (35° C), the muscles tense and the body shivers in an attempt to burn calories to generate heat. The three tried to keep warm by doing exercises, jumping jacks, and running in place. They ate candy bars for energy, but after a while they grew too tired to stay active.

"Just cuddle, kids. That's all we can do until this storm passes." Curled up in balls, the Phelan women shivered quietly as the last flame flickered out and night fell. Weary, aching, and shivering, Sandy and her daughters sat on the cold dirt floor and held each other tightly, desperately trying to share their body heat. The girls soon began shivering uncontrollably as their body temperatures slipped below normal. The snow had let up, but the wind and cold had not.

"We'll never make it to morning," Demi whimpered.

"We'll get through —" Sandy began, stopping in mid-sentence when she heard strange snickering.

Haa-haa, hee-hee, tee-hee.

"There's that giggling again!" exclaimed Lexi. She jumped up, ran to the window, and looked out into the night. The clouds had parted, allowing the faint light from a crescent moon to shine on the virgin snow. She looked out all the windows but saw no footprints or any signs of anyone.

Haa-haa, hee-hee,tee-hee.

"It sounds like they're right outside this cabin!" gasped Demi.

"So where are they?" Lexi asked. "Who are they?"

Haa-haa, hee-hee, tee-hee.

The girls tried to open the door but a high snow drift blocked it. "Whoever is out there will have to dig their way inside," said Sandy. "Otherwise in the morning we'll break a window and dig ourselves out."

"But we'll freeze to death by morning," Demi moaned.

THUMP, THUMP, THUMP.

"Somebody is definitely outside the door!" said Lexi. "Hello! Hello! We're inside. Help us!"

No one responded.

THUMP, THUMP, THUMP

"Something is falling onto the porch," said Sandy. "Let's try the door again." To their surprise the creaking old door opened easily. Then they stared at each other in open-mouthed amazement. The snow drift that minutes earlier had blocked their way was gone. A path from the doorway across the porch had been cleared.

Lexi stepped outside and happily shouted, "Look! Firewood!" Neatly stacked on the side of the door was enough chopped wood to last for several days. "Who left all this wood?"

Demi trudged around the outside of the cabin in knee-deep snow, but saw no footprints other than her own. "This is crazy. This makes no sense at all."

"The wood wasn't here before," Sandy said, "and now it is."

Haa-haa, hee-hee, tee-hee.

"Who are they?" asked Lexi. "Ghosts?"

"Look, I don't care if the snow fairy brought the wood, we're going to be warm!" Demi shouted gleefully. "We're not going to freeze to death. Let's get the wood into the cabin and build us a big, toasty-warm fire!"

Before long Sandy, Lexi, and Demi snuggled together around a roaring, crackling fire and fell into a deep sleep.

Early the next morning they were awakened by

banging on the door. "Hello!" said a deep, male voice. "Anybody here?

The Phelans jumped to their feet and opened the door to two forest rangers.

"Hi," said the taller of the two. "I'm Jack and this is my partner, Larry. We saw smoke coming out of the chimney and figured hikers had managed to break into the cabin during the storm."

"That's us," Sandy said, "but we didn't break in. The door was open."

"That's strange," said Jack. "We checked this cabin a couple of days ago and it was padlocked. Anyway, it's a good thing you got inside. I'm impressed with all the firewood you were able to chop before the storm got so bad."

"That's what's so strange," said Sandy. "We didn't chop any of it. When we found the cabin there was no firewood in sight. We were freezing. Then we heard thumps. Someone dropped this firewood off last night right after the snow stopped falling."

"At least we think it was someone," said Demi. "It could have been *something*."

"What are you talking about?" asked Jack.

"Oh," said Demi, "my crazy sister here thinks ghosts dropped the firewood off."

"We couldn't find any footprints in the snow," said Lexi. "And just before and after the thumps, we heard children laughing."

"Well, hypothermia can cause victims to imagine all sorts of wild things," said Larry.

"I can assure you," said Sandy, "that we were not

imagining things."

"How did you end up here?" asked Larry.

"We became lost while trying to find a little girl," Sandy explained. "We heard her crying but we never saw her. Then we heard another girl moaning. Finally we heard whistling, and we followed the whistle here during the storm. If it hadn't been for that, we probably would have been wandering around outside until we dropped dead from hypothermia."

"We've also been hearing kids giggling, but we've never seen any of them," Lexi added.

Larry looked at his partner. "This isn't the first time people have heard those kids. I tell you, Jack, it's connected to the Morton tragedy."

"What about the Morton tragedy?" Sandy asked.

"It's a heartbreaking story," said Larry. "Years ago, there was this family, Wade and Thelma Morton and their three kids—between eight and twelve years old. We saw them from time to time. Good kids. Happy and healthy. Their mother taught them at home. The boy was a whistler. Why, he could whistle birds out of trees and rabbits out of warrens, he was so good. Unfortunately, the father was a no-good bum. One day, in the dead of winter, he just upped and left the family. No good-byes, no nothing. He took off and deserted them.

"Thelma and the kids tried to get along as best they could, but they had no income and were running out of food. One day, in a freak storm very much like this one, Thelma got real sick. They didn't have electricity or a phone, so the boy went for help. The two girls went out for firewood. None of the kids ever came back.

"Days later a search party found their bodies. The boy had died of exposure about three miles (5 km) from the cabin. Meanwhile, the oldest girl had fallen and broken her ankle. We assume her little sister ran off to get help and got lost. They both died from exposure too. The mother survived her illness, but she was so devastated by the deaths of her children that she abandoned the cabin. She blamed her husband for the tragedy, claiming it wouldn't have happened had he not split.

"This is going to sound bizarre, but ever since the kids died, hikers in the area have reported hearing kids giggling, crying, or whistling—and they don't ever see any kids around. Sure is strange, don't you think?"

Tears began streaming down Lexi's face.

"Lexi," asked Sandy, "why are you crying?"

Lexi leaned against the wall and wiped her nose with the back of her sleeve. She began sobbing. When she was able to speak, she said, "Don't you see what's happened? We heard the ghosts of those poor little children. The three of them giggling. The moaning from the girl with the broken ankle. The pitiful cries of the little girl who was lost. And the whistler. He led us to this cabin. They had to be the ones who brought us the firewood. If it hadn't been for them helping us find shelter and giving us firewood, we would have died."

"So why are you crying so hard?" Demi asked.

"Don't you see?" said her weeping sister. "They bonded with us. We shared the same hurt. Their father deserted them just like Daddy deserted us. They didn't want us to suffer the same fate they did. They couldn't save their own lives—but they managed to save ours."

THE PHANTOM
OF THE
BAXTER MINE

Chase Duncan and his grandfather Web unloaded their camping gear directly across from the old, abandoned gold mine. Few people knew the location of the entrance, because it had been blocked by tons of rocks from a cave-in long ago. Two rusted-out balance weights and a chipped grinding stone that looked like a wheel from Fred Flintstone's car were the only clues that this was once a site sought after by men struck with gold fever.

Chase and his grandfather weren't interested in gold. They were camping out by the mine for one bizarre purpose. They hoped to catch a glimpse of the boy's great-great-great grandfather Ben—a miner who had been dead for more than 150 years.

For reasons never understood, the family history was full of stories of loved ones returning from the grave to give a message from the beyond. Usually, these ghosts would appear in their former home. But Ben's ghost was different.

According to the Duncan family legend, Ben would make his presence known only to blood relatives who held a vigil in front of the mine on the anniversary of his death. His ghost wasn't sighted every year. In fact, most years no one saw him materialize, because no one bothered to make the long, difficult hike to the old mine tucked in the northern California wilderness.

Legend also said that Ben's ghost wouldn't appear to those who were not decent and honorable, and thus worthy of the Duncan name. Many family members who made the trip to the mine didn't see him or feel his presence. They often pretended they did because they didn't want to admit they weren't worthy. Other relatives refused even to try for fear the ghost wouldn't think they were good enough to carry the Duncan name.

But ever since Chase first heard the family legend, he had wanted to see Ben for himself. For four years Chase pestered his parents to take him to the mine. Finally, when Chase was 10 years old, his grandfather Web agreed to camp out with the boy at the old mine in hopes of spotting the ghost. Web announced it would be the last time he'd attempt the vigil because he was getting too old.

The four-hour hike was tough on Web, a 63-year-old with a bad heart. Chase tried to make it as easy as possible for him. Before they headed out, Chase had switched backpacks and taken the heavier one. And although Chase was eager to get to the mine, he rested every 30 minutes because he knew his stubborn grandfather wouldn't ask for a breather.

When they arrived at the campsite, the sun had slipped

behind a ridge. Web went to the nearby stream, where he got down on his hands and knees, dunked his head in the water, and rubbed off the sweat. Then he sat on a large rock, pulled out a bandanna and wiped his bald head and leathery face.

"When do you think we'll see Ben's ghost, Gramps?" asked Chase as he dipped his own bandanna in the water and wrapped it around his neck.

"Any time between now and the morning."

"What if I don't see it?"

"Ben doesn't always make himself seen, Chase. But he does make his presence known."

"How many times have you been up here?"

"Four times."

"And you saw him every time?"

"Sometimes I saw him. Sometimes I felt his presence."

"Gramps, did he ever speak to you?"

"He doesn't talk, least he never did to me. But he communicates in his own way." Web gazed up at the sky. "It'll be dark soon. You best be getting us some firewood." Web picked up a dead branch and pulled out a pocket knife. "Now you go collect the wood while I whittle some shavings from this branch. Chase, what are the three things good firewood must be?"

"The wood must be dead, in small pieces, and lying on the ground," Chase answered.

"Exactly!" beamed Web. "I taught you well."

Once the firewood was collected, Web directed Chase on how to build it. "We'll use these shavings as our starting point. Now add the small sticks and then the thicker ones. Don't pack the wood in too tight. Fire needs air. Very good!"

The fire burned for hours and provided just enough heat to keep the night chill away. As they sat around the flickering flames long after dinner, Web poured both of them a cup of coffee to help them stay awake. Chase wasn't fond of coffee and poured four heaping teaspoons of sugar in his mug to sweeten the bitter taste. But the warm liquid felt good.

Chase could barely take his eyes off the entrance to the mine. He didn't want to miss Ben. As the night grew darker, his yearning to see the ghost grew stronger.

"Gramps, is that him?" Chase asked excitedly.

"No, Chase, it's a curious bobcat."

Minutes later: "Gramps, I think I see him!"

"No, Chase, that's tumbleweed rolling in the breeze."

Chase's false sightings continued until midnight, when tired Web crawled into their pup tent and fell asleep. Chase tossed another small log on the fire and fought to keep his tired eyes open. He swigged another cup of coffee and, under the faded light of a half moon, waited for Ben. As he stared at the mine entrance, he thought about the story of Ben Duncan.

Ben was tall and strong as an ox. Some said he could haul two timber beams on each shoulder and pull a wagonload of ore at the same time. His heart was as good as the gold he mined. A devoted husband and father of two, Ben had the respect of his co-workers and was named foreman of a mine owned by the Creed Mining Co.

At the same time, a prospector named Horace Baxter had quietly been working a mine of his own. Too cheap to hire help, Baxter used family members for several years to help him, but they quit when they realized he was cheating them out of the little gold they did find. He was such a skinflint that he shored up the tunnels with scrap timber and old posts from abandoned mines.

One day, to his boundless joy, Baxter discovered a vein of gold in his mine, one so large that he stood to become one of the richest men in America. His mind danced with all the possessions he would soon own with his fortune: a mansion filled with ornate furnishings, crystal, and gold; tailor-made clothes of the finest material; the best horses and wagons; servants, cooks, and gardeners at his beck and call. Yes, he had finally hit the jackpot.

But there was one problem. The gold was more than 400 feet (120 m) down a deep shaft, much deeper and more dangerous than where miners usually worked. Baxter needed to persuade enough miners to dig that deep and haul out his treasure. He had to find men with more skill and courage than the typical miner.

Baxter went into town where the miners were drinking coffee around a pot-bellied stove in the grocery store. He climbed onto a crate and addressed the men. "Gentlemen, my name is Horace Baxter and I have good news. I am looking for hard-working, skilled, experienced men to work for me."

"So what's the good news?" Ben Duncan asked.

"I want you men to work for me because I will pay double—that's right, double—what the other mine operators are paying you."

"What's the catch?" asked Ben.

"There is no catch. I am willing to pay top dollar for the best men to work my mine—400 feet (120 m) down."

Murmurs and whistles spread throughout the crowd.

"No wonder you're willing to pay double," said Ben as his fellow miners nodded and grunted in agreement. "Who wants to go down that far to dig? It's not safe. No amount of money is worth working for if a man doesn't come up at the end of the day to collect."

Baxter was surprised and worried that none of the miners jumped at the chance to double their salary. Here he was, sitting on a fortune and willing to pay good money for men to dig it up for him, and they weren't eager.

"It doesn't matter how deep the mine is," said Baxter. "Whether it's 100 (30 m) or 400 (120 m) feet under the ground. You just brace the roofs of those tunnels with good, hefty timber and you dig out the gold the same way you're doing now. I've been down in my mine many times, and I've got the finest timbers and braces money can buy."

Baxter was lying through his teeth, but he flashed a big smile and said, "All right, men, sign up over here if you want to go to work for me and get rich."

"Mr. Baxter," said Ben, "if you have the safest mine like you say you have—and I have no reason to doubt you—then there's no danger in working in your mine, right?"

"That's right," replied Baxter. "Now you're talking sense. Why, it's the safest mine you'll ever see."

Ben walked up to Baxter, held out his hand and said, "All right, I'll come work for you—but on one condition. If I happen to get buried down there in your mine, you agree to pay my wife one thousand dollars."

"I'll do better than that, mister. In the unlikely event that you die in a mishap in my mine, I'll personally pay her *two thousand* dollars!"

The miners whooped and cheered. Back then, that was more than two years' salary. Led by Ben, the miners, including Ben's three younger brothers, Tom, Fred, and Clay, quit their jobs and signed up to work in the Baxter Mine. Soon the men were bringing up large quantities of gold-laden ore. It was hard, dirty work. The men were working with hand tools in narrow shafts and tunnels only five feet (1.5 m) high. They toiled in two-man teams of a shaker and a driller. The shaker held a star drill, a steel rod with one end tapered and sharpened into the shape of a star. He placed it against the hard rock while the driller struck it with a sledgehammer. The shaker then cleared the chipped rock after each stroke.

Although Ben was making good money, his wife, Reba, had a bad feeling about him working in the Baxter Mine. But Ben assured her he would be extra careful. He also tried to sweet-talk her with dreams of earning enough to have his own mine, hitting it rich, and giving her a wonderful life.

With his big pay increase Ben bought his wife and kids little gifts. But still Reba worried. After trying to ease her mind once again, Ben grinned and said, "Why, honey, if anything did happen to me, you'd be a rich lady. Horace Baxter promised me he'd pay you two thousand dollars."

The weeks passed without any safety problems and, although Reba's mind was never at rest, at least her fears were eased.

But then one rainy evening Ben didn't come home for dinner. It wasn't like him to be late. On the rare times he was, he always sent word to Reba so she wouldn't worry.

But no word came. As night fell, Reba, her heart seized by worry, gathered her two young sons and hurried over to the home of Ben's brother Tom, Chase's great-great-great uncle.

"Have you seen Ben?" asked Reba, almost pleading that the answer would be yes. "He didn't show up for dinner and I'm worried sick."

"No, Reba," Tom replied. "I last saw him at quitting time. He was still in the mine. He said he needed to check on the braces of a tunnel and then would be on his way."

Reba draped her arms around Tom's neck and broke down in tears. "Ben is still down there!" she wailed. "I know he is. He's had an accident or he'd be home by now. Get him out, Tom. Please!"

"Okay, Reba, okay. I'll round up my brothers and we'll go check the mine. I'm sure he's fine. He probably had a meeting with Mr. Baxter that took longer than he thought."

But in his heart Tom knew better. He didn't tell Reba about the dream he just had when he had dozed off in front of the fire right after dinner. In the dream he saw a tunnel collapse and heard an anguished shout. Someone was buried under the rubble. Tom had awakened from his dream when Reba knocked on his door.

Now Tom fought the dreaded thought that his brother was dead. He and Ben, who was a year older, were very close. They often knew what the other was thinking without saying a word. *Could the dream have been a fateful message from his brother?* he wondered.

Tom quickly rounded up his two younger brothers, Fred and Clay, and headed out in the raw, wet night to the Baxter Mine. When they reached the entrance they lit their lanterns and started down the deep shaft to one of the tunnels the miners had been working in that day.

"Ben! Are you down here?" shouted Tom. "Ben! Answer me!" But all he heard was his own muffled echo bouncing off the rock walls. He and his brothers searched every inch of the tunnel, but found no sign of any collapse.

The next morning, Reba, her eyes red and her hands trembling, went into Baxter's office, begging him to launch a full-scale search of the entire mine and all its tunnels. But he refused, asserting that Ben probably took off for a day or two "for his own reasons" and would return.

Reba and the Duncan brothers knew that Ben would never do such a thing. The brothers searched several other tunnels without success.

That night Tom was tossing and turning in bed when he heard a loud rapping at the front door. He stumbled sleepily to the door and opened it. "Oh my gosh!" Tom cried out. "It's you!"

Standing before him was Ben, his pasty-white face caked in dust and blood. His dark sunken eyes were filled with anguish.

"You're alive!" Tom rushed forward to hug his beloved brother. But to Tom's shock, his arms went right through Ben. All he felt was a strange chill in the space occupied by his brother.

Tom gasped and backed away. "I—I don't understand."

"I'm dead, Tom."

"You're a ghost?" Tom gasped in disbelief. "I must be having a nightmare." Tom covered his eyes and cried out in horror.

"Tom, gather yourself!" ordered Ben. "You're my brother and now you won't even look at me?"

Tom let his hands drop down to his sides and opened his eyes. "I—I'm sorry, Ben."

"Are you going to leave me down in the dark and the damp forever?"

"But we tried to find you. We went looking for you last night and today."

"I heard you, Tom. But you went too deep. Stop at the second tunnel and go in. At the fork turn to the left. You'll find me."

"What happened to you, Ben?"

"I was examining the timber in the tunnel. It's cheap wood, Tom. It's not safe. I was heading out when the timber gave way and buried me. Please get me out of there."

"I promise. I'll do it right now!"

"Thanks, Tom. I knew I could count on you." And then, without moving a step, Ben slowly faded away.

Tom stood still, trying to collect his thoughts. His head and heart swirled in a whirlwind of grief over his brother's death and the shock of seeing Ben's ghost. When he finally recovered, Tom told his two younger brothers of his astounding encounter with Ben's ghost. No matter how crazy the story sounded, the Duncan brothers were not prone to make up tales, especially one so tragic. Within minutes the three Duncan brothers had raced to the Baxter Mine.

Tom led the men down the shaft and into the tunnel. They reached the fork and turned left. After walking another 200 feet (60 m), they saw the cave-in; the tunnel was blocked by fallen timber and rock.

"I've been waiting for you, my brothers," said Ben.

Fred and Clay couldn't believe their eyes. The ghost of their brother Ben stood forlornly beside the rubble. He looked just as pale, bloody, and dirty as he did when he appeared at Tom's house.

"Are you really dead?" Fred asked tearfully.

"Yes. I am buried under this debris about ten feet (3 m) farther in. And I have Baxter to blame. He lied. The mine isn't safe, and it never will be, because he used cheap timbers. A lot of them are rotten. There will be more cave-ins because the braces won't hold. That's what happened to me. One of them just gave way, it was so rotten.

"Tell Baxter I will haunt this mine so that no one will ever step foot in it again. No one should die needlessly to feed the greed of one man."

Ben began to fade away.

"Wait, don't go," pleaded Tom. "Will we ever see you again?"

"Only to those like you, my brothers, whose hearts are filled with decency, honesty, and compassion." And then Ben vanished.

The miners dug furiously. Soon Tom's shovel struck metal. Clearing the rock, he saw a hand wrapped around the handle of a pick axe. Dropping to their knees, the men scooped out rocks and dirt until they uncovered Ben's body. Cradling it in his arms, Tom tearfully carried the body to the surface and then home to Ben's grieving widow Reba.

The next morning Tom went to Baxter's office and said, "Ben Duncan is home. You need to see him now."

"I told you Ben would show up," said Baxter. "But I'm busy. I can't go now."

"Yes you can," Tom replied. "It's important."

Grumbling, Baxter walked with Tom, who refused to say another word. When the two arrived at Ben's house, miners were milling around, silent and sad.

"What's going on?" asked Baxter.

"Just get inside the house," said Tom. He held the door open and Baxter walked in. At one end of the room was a pine coffin. Baxter didn't need to get any closer to know it held the body of Ben Duncan. He walked over to Reba, who was sitting in a rocker, clutching her two small children.

"I'm so sorry, Mrs. Duncan. Ben was a good man."

Without looking up at him, she nodded.

"You owe her an apology—and money," Tom demanded.

Gazing at the angry looks of the miners who had crowded into the room, Baxter said, "I should have known that Ben wouldn't run off for a few days. I apologize."

"No," growled Tom, "apologize about the lies you've told us about the safety of the mine."

"I have no further apologies to make," countered Baxter. "Now then, Mrs. Duncan, as for the money, I will give you the thousand dollars in my office."

Angry shouts of protest rose from the men. "You promised *two* thousand dollars," charged Fred. "We were all in the store the day you hired Ben. We all heard you say his widow would get two grand if he should die in the mine."

The men started to close in on Baxter, who held up his hands and smiled nervously. "I guess I was mistaken. You're right. It was two thousand."

Later that afternoon Tom escorted Reba to Baxter's office and collected the money.

Led by the surviving Duncan brothers, the miners refused to go back to work, claiming the mine was unsafe. Baxter stood at the mine entrance and pleaded with them. "You're making a big mistake if you quit," he said. "This mine is perfectly safe. I'll give each man a 50 percent raise in pay. So come on back to work."

"Ben said this mine is unsafe, and that's all we need to hear," shouted Clay.

"When did he say such a thing?"

"After his death!"

"His ghost told you that?" asked Baxter in disbelief.

"Yes, and he promised to haunt this mine forever," added Fred. "No one will ever work in there again. It's not worth taking another human life."

With that said, Tom, Fred, and Clay and the rest of the miners turned on their heels and stormed off. Word spread throughout the region that the Baxter Mine was haunted and always would be. No miner would work for Baxter again—especially because the ghost of Ben Duncan said it was unsafe.

Baxter tried everything to get men to work for him. But it was futile. He had crossed too many people.

In desperation, Baxter decided to go in the mine and dig out the gold with his own hands. But moments before he started down, he heard a muffled roar. Billowing dust poured out of the entrance. Baxter dropped to his knees and wept. The mine's tunnels, weakened by the rotten, cheap timber he had used, had collapsed one by one. The cave-ins buried once and for all Baxter's dream of striking it rich.

From that day on the sealed mine became a ghostly shrine to the Duncan family, a reminder of the decency and honesty of Ben Duncan.

"Well, Chase, did you see Ben's ghost?"

"Huh? What?" mumbled Chase. He shielded his eyes from the early morning sun and groaned. "Oh, no, Gramps. I must have fallen asleep. I missed him!"

"Don't fret. The morning isn't over yet. Let's go for a dip in the stream."

Dejected and angry at himself, Chase glumly stripped down to his shorts and waded in the cold mountain water.

"I must not be worthy," Chase groused. "Ben didn't show himself to me."

"Are you worthy only if someone else says you are?"

"Uh, I guess not, Gramps."

"Do you feel you're worthy?"

"I think so."

"You *think*?" scoffed Web. "Don't you know?"

"Well, I'm honest and I try to be kind to people. So, yes, I am worthy. But it sure would have been nice to have Ben Duncan's ghost confirm it."

Chase returned to the campsite and put on his pants and shirt. As he slipped his right foot into his hiking boot, he let out a yelp. "There's something hard in my boot." He yanked his foot out, reached in, and pulled out a small rock that sparkled in the sun. "What's this?"

Web stepped out of the stream, walked over to Chase, and held the rock up to the morning light.

"It's plain to me, son. This is a gold nugget."

"But how did it get in my boot?"

Suddenly a large rock tumbled down from the top of the mine entrance, striking another rock and lodging between two boulders.

Gramps stared at the entrance and said, "There's your answer."

The sun's rays had struck the boulders in such a way that the shadows between the rocks at the entrance formed two clearly defined letters.

"B. D!" shouted Chase. "Ben Duncan! The gold nugget and the initials in the shadows must be his way of communicating with me! Gramps, the ghost thinks I'm worthy!"

Web nodded and threw his arm around his grandson. "I guess old Ben does think you're worthy. But then, we already knew that, didn't we?"

THE SKULL OF LEAPING BUFFALO

If Cassie Mooney and Emily Tyson had known what terror lay ahead of them, they never, ever would have taken the human skull out of the ground. They would have left it buried with the rest of the bones in a grave that had remained untouched for over a century.

They thought the skull was the centerpiece of a practical joke. Who knew it would bring such terror?

Cassie and Emily belonged to a high school project involving science students who spent a weekend camping out in the Black Hills of South Dakota. The dozen students, under the guidance of teacher Kent Olson, searched for fossils, mineral samples, and Native American artifacts.

After setting up their camp, Mr. Olson gathered the students around the campfire for a brief lecture. "The Black Hills were formed millions of years ago when pressure from below raised the crust of the earth into a dome 50 miles (80 km) wide," the teacher explained. "Erosion wore this dome into gigantic rock stubs, which we now call the Black Hills. How did this area get its name?"

Cassie raised her hand and answered, "Because the slopes were covered with thick pine forests. The area looked black to the Sioux Indians when seen from the plains."

"Very good, Cassie," commended Mr. Olson.

Emily, who was sitting next to Cassie, playfully poked her in the ribs and whispered mockingly, "Very good, Cassie. Mr. Olson didn't bring his dog along, because he has you as teacher's pet."

In spirited retaliation, Cassie yanked on Emily's blond ponytail, which was poking out of her baseball cap.

Emily yelped in pain and cried, "Ow! You ripped out my hair!"

Cassie uttered an even louder shriek when she realized she held Emily's ponytail in her hand. Cassie held it up as if it were a dead mouse and then flung it to the ground in alarm.

Meanwhile, Emily couldn't contain herself any longer and burst out laughing. "Gotcha!"

"What?" asked her wide-eyed friend.

"It's a hair extension. I've been waiting all day to play that joke on you!"

Emily's laughter came to an abrupt halt when she saw Mr. Olson standing over them. "Ladies, I love your sense of humor. You two are the school's most notorious practical jokers. But there's a time and place for everything. Right now we're here to learn. Later you can laugh your heads off. Okay?"

"Yes, Mr. Olson," they replied in unison.

"Now then," said the teacher, addressing the entire

group, "the Black Hills were once part of a reservation for the Sioux Indians. But thousands of white settlers poured into the area after gold was discovered in 1874 . . ."

Before the students went into their two-person tents for the night, Cassie reminded her classmates, "Don't forget to zip up your tents. You don't want any creepy crawlies like recluse spiders or scorpions to sneak in and bite you. They're active at this time of year."

Later, after the fire had been doused and the giggling and talking in the tents had quieted down, Cassie told Emily, "Look at your watch. Let's see how long it takes for Bobby or Mick to fly out of their tent."

"What did you do, Cassie?" Emily asked eagerly.

"See this string, here? It goes to their tent. When I pull on it, a plastic scorpion will fall onto one of their sleeping bags." She yanked on the string. "I think it will take under ten seconds."

Resting on their knees the girls peeked out of their tent and waited. Six seconds, seven, eight . . .

"Yeow! Scorpion!" Bobby tore out of the tent with Mick at his heels. Then Bobby grabbed a shoe and cautiously went back inside while Mick held the lantern. WHAM! "I got it!"

After a moment of silence the boys began to bellow. "It's a fake! We've been duped! Mooney and Tyson, we'll get you for this!"

"We don't know what you're talking about," snickered Cassie as the girls giggled and closed the flap to their tent.

The next day the students split into two-person groups and scoured the area looking for fossils, artifacts, and samples of beryl, feldspar, gypsum, and mica.

"Which way are you girls going?" Bobby asked Cassie and Emily. Cassie pointed to a hill a few hundred yards from the camp.

"Be careful, Mooney," Mick warned. "You never know what you might dig up."

As the boys walked off, Bobby put his arm on Mick's shoulder and said, "Hey, Mick, do you know what *skullduggery* means?" They looked at the girls and laughed.

"What was that all about?" Emily asked Cassie.

Cassie shrugged her shoulders. "Who knows? Boys."

The girls headed off on their own, hoping to fill their bag with samples for the science lab. As they snooped around, Cassie noticed a gray, triangular-shaped object between two rocks. She reached down and pulled it out. It was a stone that had been chiseled into a sharp point.

"An arrowhead!" said Emily. "Way to go, Cassie."

"Where there's one, there's two," said Cassie. They got down on their knees, moved rocks, and brushed off the dirt. As their search intensified, Cassie came across a smooth, round, yellowish object. It had a slight crack across the top. With her trowel, she carved out more dirt. It was starting to take the shape of ...of ...

Cassie's heart began to pound faster. *This is not a stone, but I think I know what it is,* she told herself, fighting off a shiver. *Two large holes in the front, two smaller ones on each side...*"Oh my gosh! Emily! Oh my gosh!" Cassie screamed and dropped her trowel.

Emily ran to her side and then backed off when she saw it. "Oh!" she yelped with a shudder. "It's a skull! A human skull!"

"Don't touch it, Emily. Remember what Mr. Olson said. If we find any fossils, we're supposed to call him first."

"Do you suppose it's a murder victim?"

"I don't know, but we better get Mr. Olson."

They started back to the camp when Emily grabbed Cassie by the arm. "Wait a minute. What's the matter with us? That skull isn't real. I'll bet you anything that Bobby and Mick planted it to scare us."

Cassie hit her forehead with her hand. "Of course! They all but told us. Remember when Bobby asked Mick if he knew what skullduggery means?"

"So what are we going to do?"

Cassie picked up the skull, brushed off the caked dirt, and held it out as if admiring a piece of fine art. "This skull will make the perfect centerpiece for a joke. We'll get even with those boys."

"But Cassie, we got them first and then they got us, so we're even now."

"We women always need to be one step ahead of the guys." She put the skull in her canvas bag. "Don't say a word about the skull to anyone, okay?"

When all the students regrouped at the camp later that day, Bobby went up to the two girls and asked, "Well, Mooney and Tyson, did you find anything interesting today?"

"A couple of arrowheads," Emily replied.

Cassie added good-naturedly, "And rocks—you know, the kind that are in your head."

That night, as the students and Mr. Olson sat around the campfire, the group traded ghost stories. When it was Cassie's turn, she said, "This isn't really a story. It's a fact.

During a war between the Sioux and Arikara Indians near here in the 1830s, a Sioux got his head chopped off. The Arikara skinned it and took it back to their camp as a trophy. They stuck the skull on a pole and danced around it. Boy, were they sorry they did! The next morning the skull was gone, and they didn't know what had happened to it."

Cassie paused in the middle of this whopper for dramatic effect and gazed into the eyes of each of her fellow students. "The skull made the Arikara wish they had never gone to war. In the middle of the night it would float right into their tepees and let out a bloodcurdling scream before it disappeared into the darkness. The skull haunted them night after night until they couldn't stand it anymore. The Arikara fled to another area, but it was no use. The skull followed them from place to place and tortured them with its haunting screams.

"I hear some snickering among you disbelievers. I feel it is my duty to inform you that the skull has never rested. Over the years, prospectors, campers, and even scientists have seen and heard the screaming skull. Who knows? It could show up tonight—in your very tent."

Everyone in the group laughed and clapped. "Quite a story, Cassie, and you did it with a straight face," marveled Mr. Olson. He stood up, yawned, and stretched his arms. "Well, gang, it's getting late. Let's turn in. You know the rules: no visitors in your tent at night—and that goes for screaming skulls."

Later, as the girls snuggled into their sleeping bags, Emily asked Cassie, "Are we going to scare the boys with the skull tonight?"

"Nah, they'll be expecting us to do something. We'll catch them off-guard tomorrow night. I'm tired. See you in the morning, Emily."

At about 2 A.M. Cassie was awakened from a sound sleep by strange tinkling beside her head. "Is that you, Emily?" Cassie flicked on her flashlight, saw Emily was asleep, and then aimed the light next to her sleeping bag. The beam caught an unexpectedly strange sight. Small black stones, all less than an inch in diameter, were slowly falling to the floor like snowflakes.

"Bobby and Mick!" Cassie muttered to herself. She shined her light onto the ceiling of the tent. "What in the world is going on here?" To her amazement, the last two black stones looked as if they had come from outside the tent and fallen through the top of the tent—even though there was no hole in the ceiling. "How did they do that?" She waited for more stones to fall, but none did.

Cassie slipped out of her tent expecting to find Bobby or Mick. But they weren't there. She crept over to their tent and heard one of them snoring.

Cassie returned to her tent only to discover that the mysterious tiny stones were lightly falling once again. She held out her hand to catch one of them. Unbelievably, she couldn't snare a single one. Just as one was about to land in the palm of her hand, it changed direction in midair and floated away. By now several dozen had piled up on the floor of the tent.

"Emily," she called out excitedly. "Wake up! Look!"

"Huh? What's going on? Is it morning already?"

"Look up at the ceiling. What do you see?"

"Oh, my gosh," said Emily, rubbing her eyes. "Let's kill it!"

Cassie gazed up and saw a large, furry spider crawling near the spot where the stones had been falling. "No, not the spider. I'm talking about the falling stones."

"What stones?"

The stones had stopped floating down. "Emily, stones were falling from our ceiling. Here, look for yourself." Cassie scooped up several stones that had collected by the head of her sleeping bag and handed them to her.

Emily sifted them through her fingers. "They're warm. They feel like little bits of smooth granite. Where did you get them?"

"I already told you. They fell from the ceiling."

"Right," Emily said sarcastically. "It's too late for another one of your jokes." Before rolling over, she grumbled, "Get some sleep, Cassie, and turn off the light."

Cassie flicked off the flashlight, but she didn't get back to sleep. *I can't be dreaming,* she thought. *I mean, the stones are right here. I saw them falling. I can't wait to show them to Mr. Olson in the morning.*

Just then the most terrible yell that ever rattled the stillness of the night assaulted her ears.

AAAHHH-OOOWWW-RRRR.

It sounded like a cross between coyotes howling and lions roaring. "Emily, did you hear that?"

Emily grunted a few times and then moaned, "Cassie, will you shut up and let me sleep."

"Just listen for a moment."

Irritated, Emily sat up in her sleeping bag. "I don't hear

a thing. Now quit bothering me." Emily plopped down and rolled over. Then she zipped her sleeping bag up to her head and scrunched farther down so she was completely inside.

Cassie couldn't lie down. Her mind was whirring in a mad scramble, searching for any explanation, no matter how far-fetched, for the falling stones and the frightening yell.

AAAHHH-OOOWWW-RRRR.

Cassie jumped up. "Emily, you heard that, didn't you?"

But Emily wasn't responding.

AAAHHH-OOOWWW-RRRR.

The unearthly yell jangled Cassie's nerves and pumped fear into her veins. *Is that the noise of animals fighting?* she wondered. *Maybe. But it sounds as if it's right outside this tent! What is it? Wait a minute—*Cassie pounded her fist on the floor of the tent. *It's those boys again! Well, the fun and games are over.* Cassie charged out of her tent and began to march toward the neighboring tent when she stopped dead in her tracks. She gasped.

In front of her stood a muscular Indian staring at her with angry eyes that seemed to bore right through her. From the flickering light of the dying fire she saw his leathery face form a scowl. Two long, jet-black braids drooped down to his thick shoulders. He was clad in an open vest, pants, and moccasins all made from deerskin.

"Who are you?" asked Cassie, speaking loudly in the hopes that someone else would hear her.

"I go by the name of Leaping Buffalo," replied the Indian in a deep monotone.

Cassie burst out laughing. "You're making this up. I don't believe you."

"Do you not believe your eyes when they see stones fall like snowflakes from nowhere? Do you not believe your ears when they hear the yell of angry spirits inside your head?"

"I must admit those are pretty cool tricks."

The Indian grunted in disgust. "I have little time to talk. I must soon go," he said. "I come to tell you of a wrong that has been done to me. It must be made right, or you will face the consequences."

"This is a joke, right?" asked Cassie, forcing a smile. "Did Bobby or Mick put you up to this?"

"I am here because of your own misdeed."

"My misdeed? What did I do?"

"You have done what too many others have done for far too long. For centuries my people lived in harmony with the land. The plains were black with buffalo. The mountains were dark with trees. The streams were pure. We hunted and fished and grew crops to feed, clothe, and shelter our families. But then the white man mortally wounded our way of life, our customs, our beliefs. He grabbed the land for himself, broke promises to the Indian, and plunged us into hunger, sickness, and despair. Look around you. Now nothing remains to mark the place where once dwelt a mighty people. Nothing has remained sacred of what was once sacred. Not even in death can we find peace. My troubled spirit has had an uneasy rest. Unsettled though it was for so many years, at least it was at rest—until you disturbed it."

"What are you talking about?"

"Today you found my skull and carried it away. You stole a part of me. You have committed an offense against my grave. The skull must be returned to its resting place."

"I don't have your skull," said Cassie. "The only skull I have is a fake one. Here, I'll show you."

She went into her tent, fumbled around in her canvas bag, and pulled out the skull. She returned outside, but the Indian had vanished.

Cassie suddenly felt a wave of embarrassment building up inside her. *This is definitely a prank,* she thought. *The boys got me real good. She looked at her watch. It was close to 3 A.M. I'm being played for a fool, and I fell for this gag like a sucker. They must be watching me from their tents.*

After tossing the skull into her tent, she scurried around several of the other tents and a few large boulders and bushes on the perimeter of the campsite, but found no witnesses. *Hey, what gives? It's no fun pulling off a prank if you can't see it. I could go back into the tent and pretend it never happened. But, hey, I'm a good sport. If they really are asleep, then maybe they should be up. After all, their prank got me up at 3 A.M.*

Cassie walked over to Bobby and Mick's tent and said, "Congratulations, guys. I admit, you got me good."

"Mooney, is that you?" mumbled Bobby. "What do you want at this hour?"

"The skull gag," she replied. "Very good."

"Oh, you found it. Glad you liked it. You didn't say anything about it when you returned to the camp. We

thought you missed it. But, you know, it's three in the morning. Can we talk about this later, like when normal people wake up?"

"No way. I've got to know. Where did you get the Indian? And the stones. That one has me stumped."

"Indian? Stones? Go to sleep."

From another tent came an annoyed voice, "Hey, quiet out there. We're trying to sleep."

Cassie lowered her voice, but raised the intensity of her tone. "All right, Bobby, you asked for it. I'm coming in there!"

"Hey, get out of here!" squealed Bobby as Cassie threw back the tent flap and hopped inside.

Mick sat up in his sleeping bag and barked, "What are you doing, Mooney? You're going to get us all in trouble."

Cassie grabbed a shoe from each of the boys and threatened, "So help me, guys, I'll throw these shoes over the nearest cliff if you don't come clean. Tell me exactly how you pulled off the joke with the stones and the Indian."

"Cassie, you're goofy," said Mick. "The skull joke we admit. But we don't know anything about stones or an Indian."

Frustrated, Cassie tossed the shoes at the boys and stormed back into her tent. As she lay on top of her sleeping bag she turned on the flashlight and aimed it up at the ceiling, trying to find the hole the stones had fallen through. Suddenly her eyes grew in stark terror.

Directly in front of her floated the head of a monster! Glistening, razor-sharp horns jutted out from thick, matted black hair. Menacing white eyes glared in hatred as a flat, wide nose snorted in disdain. Fat, white lips formed a squared-off mouth that blew foul air into Cassie's face.

Petrified by the unbelievable sight, Cassie tried to scream but nothing came out of her throat. She couldn't even move her hand to wake up Emily. Only her eyes moved as they watched the horrible monster face float closer and closer, until it hovered just inches away from her. The awful snorting and sickening smell of its hot breath was suffocating the terror-stricken teen until her brain and body could no longer cope.

Cassie passed out.

"Cassie, wake up," said Emily, gently shaking her friend. "It's 6:30. Everybody's up but you. Come on."

Cassie opened her eyes, stared blankly at Emily, and let out a bone-jarring scream. Mr. Olson and the other kids dashed to the front of the tent. By now Cassie had regained her senses and felt sheepish about her scream. "I think I had a nightmare," she murmured. "I'm sorry."

After Cassie described the floating monster head, Mr. Olson, who was kneeling by her side, said, "It sounds like a mask worn by Plains Indians when they do the buffalo dance. They make the mask out of a buffalo scalp and horns. While they do the buffalo dance they ask the great spirit for a successful hunt." He then sniffed the air. "No offense, Cassie, but it kind of smells like a buffalo was in here."

She inhaled too and then clutched her teacher's hand. "Mr. Olson, the floating head had the same foul smell. What if it wasn't a dream?"

"What?" he asked, shaking his head.

Cassie grabbed a handful of stones that had fallen earlier that night. "What about these? I saw them falling from the roof of my tent—even though there was no hole!"

"Emily," Mr. Olson said, "did you see the monster and the falling stones too?"

"Neither," she replied. "I was asleep. But when Cassie woke me up, I felt the stones and they were warm."

"These stones are the kind once used by the Sioux. They put them in gourds for ceremonial dances. I don't have a clue how these stones got into your tent."

"Mr. Olson," said Cassie worriedly. "There was this Indian outside saying I had stolen his skull and that he wanted it back." She pointed to the skull sitting in the corner.

The teacher picked it up and examined it. "Where did you get this?"

"Over by that tall hill a few hundred yards from here. It was near where we found the arrowheads."

"Why didn't you tell me, Cassie?" asked Mr. Olson. "I thought I made it very clear to everyone that you were not to touch any bones or fossils."

"But this is a fake, a joke from Bobby and Mick."

"Cassie, this is no fake," asserted the teacher, fingering the skull. "This is a real human skull."

Mr. Olson, followed by Cassie, left the tent and confronted Bobby and Mick. "Where did you get this skull?"

"That's not ours, Mr. Olson," said Bobby. "We never saw that one before."

"Here's the one we used as a joke on Mooney," said Mick. He held up the sun-bleached skull of a cow. It had lipstick painted around the mouth and charcoal-drawn eyebrows and eyelashes. Printed across the forehead was the name *MOOOOney*. "We put the cow skull on a stick and left it on the hillside. We figured Cassie would find it there. When she didn't bring it back to the camp or say anything about it, we went out and brought it back."

Cassie's head was swimming in a unpleasant mixture of dismay and bewilderment. "Mr. Olson, I think I'm going to be sick," she moaned. "If the human skull was real, then maybe everything else that happened to me last night was real too. The Indian wanted his skull back, so he used some hocus-pocus to convince me he was real. When I didn't believe him because I still thought it was a joke, he scared me with the floating buffalo mask."

"Cassie, that's an incredible story—even for you and your gifted imagination," said Mr. Olson. "But far be it from me to say you're wrong. Believe what you want. In the meantime, let's return this skull to its original resting place."

"I'm all for that," Cassie sighed. "It's the only way I'll ever rest again."